Love Stories

By

Mary Roberts Rinehart

LOVE STORIES

TWENTY-TWO

I

The Probationer's name was really Nella Jane Brown, but she was entered in the training school as N. Jane Brown. However, she meant when she was accepted to be plain Jane Brown. Not, of course, that she could ever be really plain.

People on the outside of hospitals have a curious theory about nurses, especially if they are under twenty. They believe that they have been disappointed in love. They never think that they may intend to study medicine later on, or that they may think nursing is a good and honourable career, or that they may really like to care for the sick.

The man in this story had the theory very hard.

When he opened his eyes after the wall of the warehouse dropped, N. Jane Brown was sitting beside him. She had been practising counting pulses on him, and her eyes were slightly upturned and very earnest.

There was a strong odour of burnt rags in the air, and the man sniffed. Then he put a hand to his upper lip—the right hand. She was holding his left.

"Did I lose anything besides this?" he inquired. His little moustache was almost entirely gone. A gust of fire had accompanied the wall.

"Your eyebrows," said Jane Brown.

The man—he was as young for a man as Jane Brown was for a nurse—the man lay quite still for a moment. Then:

"I'm sorry to undeceive you," he said. "But my right leg is off."

He said it lightly, because that is the way he took things. But he had a strange singing in his ears.

"I'm afraid it's broken. But you still have it." She smiled. She had a very friendly smile. "Have you any pain anywhere?"

He was terribly afraid she would go away and leave him, so, although he was quite comfortable, owing to a hypodermic he had had, he groaned slightly. He was, at that time, not particularly interested in Jane Brown, but he did not want to be alone. He closed his eyes and said feebly:

"Water!"

She gave him a teaspoonful, bending over him and being careful not to spill it down his neck. Her uniform crackled when she moved. It had rather too much starch in it.

The man, whose name was Middleton, closed his eyes. Owing to the morphia, he had at least a hundred things he wished to discuss. The trouble was to fix on one out of the lot.

"I feel like a bit of conversation," he observed. "How about you?"

Then he saw that she was busy again. She held an old-fashioned hunting-case watch in her hand, and her eyes were fixed on his chest. At each rise and fall of the coverlet her lips moved. Mr. Middleton, who was feeling wonderful, experimented. He drew four very rapid breaths, and four very slow ones. He was rewarded by seeing her rush to a table and write something on a sheet of yellow paper.

"Resparation, very iregular," was what she wrote. She was not a particularly good speller.

After that Mr. Middleton slept for what he felt was a day and a night. It was really ten minutes by the hunting-case watch. Just long enough for the Senior Surgical Interne, known in the school as the S.S.I., to wander in, feel his pulse, approve of Jane Brown, and go out.

Jane Brown had risen nervously when he came in, and had proffered him the order book and a clean towel, as she had been instructed. He had, however, required neither. He glanced over the record, changed the spelling of "resparation," arranged his tie at the mirror, took another look at Jane Brown, and went out. He had not spoken.

It was when his white-linen clad figure went out that Middleton wakened and found it was the same day. He felt at once like conversation, and he began immediately. But the morphia did a curious thing to him. He was never afterward able to explain it. It made him create. He lay there and invented for Jane Brown a fictitious person, who was himself. This person, he said, was a newspaper reporter, who had been sent to report the warehouse fire. He had got too close, and a wall had come down on him. He invented the newspaper, too, but, as Jane Brown had come from somewhere else, she did not notice this.

In fact, after a time he felt that she was not as really interested as she might have been, so he introduced a love element. He was, as has been said, of those who believe that nurses go into hospitals because of being blighted. So he introduced a Mabel, suppressing her other name, and boasted, in a way he afterward remembered with horror, that Mabel was in love with him. She was, he related, something or other on his paper.

At the end of two hours of babbling, a businesslike person in a cap—the Probationer wears no cap—relieved Jane Brown, and spilled some beef tea down his neck.

Now, Mr. Middleton knew no one in that city. He had been motoring through, and he had, on seeing the warehouse burning, abandoned his machine for a closer view. He had left it with the engine running, and, as a matter of fact, it ran for four hours, when it died of starvation, and was subsequently interred in a city garage. However, he owned a number of cars, so he wasted no thought on that one. He was a great deal more worried about his eyebrows, and, naturally, about his leg.

When he had been in the hospital ten hours it occurred to him to notify his family. But he put it off for two reasons: first, it would be a lot of trouble; second, he had no reason to think they particularly wanted to know. They all had such a lot of things to do, such as bridge and opening country houses and going to the Springs. They were really overwhelmed, without anything new, and they had never been awfully interested in him anyhow.

He was not at all bitter about it.

That night Mr. Middleton — but he was now officially "Twenty-two," by that system of metonymy which designates a hospital private patient by the number of his room — that night "Twenty-two" had rather a bad time, between his leg and his conscience. Both carried on disgracefully. His leg stabbed, and his conscience reminded him of Mabel, and that if one is going to lie, there should at least be a reason. To lie out of the whole cloth — —!

However, toward morning, with what he felt was the entire pharmacopœia inside him, and his tongue feeling like a tar roof, he made up his mind to stick to his story, at least as far as the young lady with the old-fashioned watch was concerned. He had a sort of creed, which shows how young he was, that one should never explain to a girl.

There was another reason still. There had been a faint sparkle in the eyes of the young lady with the watch while he was lying to her. He felt that she was seeing him in heroic guise, and the thought pleased him. It was novel.

To tell the truth, he had been getting awfully bored with himself since he left college. Everything he tried to do, somebody else could do so much better. And he comforted himself with this, that he would have been a journalist if he could, or at least have published a newspaper. He knew what was wrong with about a hundred newspapers.

He decided to confess about Mabel, but to hold fast to journalism. Then he lay in bed and watched for the Probationer to come back.

However, here things began to go wrong. He did not see Jane Brown again. There were day nurses and night nurses and reliefs, and internes and Staff and the Head Nurse and the First Assistant and—everything but Jane Brown. And at last he inquired for her.

"The first day I was in here," he said to Miss Willoughby, "there was a little girl here without a cap. I don't know her name. But I haven't seen her since."

Miss Willoughby, who, if she had been disappointed in love, had certainly had time to forget it, Miss Willoughby reflected.

"Without a cap? Then it was only one of the probationers."

"You don't remember which one?"

But she only observed that probationers were always coming and going, and it wasn't worth while learning their names until they were accepted. And that, anyhow, probationers should never be sent to private patients, who are paying a lot and want the best.

"Really," she added, "I don't know what the school is coming to. Since this war in Europe every girl wants to wear a uniform and be ready to go to the front if we have trouble. All sorts of silly children are applying. We have one now, on this very floor, not a day over nineteen."

"Who is she?" asked Middleton. He felt that this was the one. She was so exactly the sort Miss Willoughby would object to.

"Jane Brown," snapped Miss Willoughby. "A little, namby-pamby, mush-and-milk creature, afraid of her own shadow."

Now, Jane Brown, at that particular moment, was sitting in her little room in the dormitory, with the old watch ticking on the stand so she would not over-stay her off duty. She was aching with fatigue from her head, with its smooth and shiny hair, to her feet, which were in a bowl of witch hazel and hot water. And she was crying over a letter she was writing.

Jane Brown had just come from her first death. It had taken place in H ward, where she daily washed window-sills, and disinfected stands, and carried dishes in and out. And it had not been what she had expected. In the first place, the man had died for hours. She had never heard of this. She had thought of death as coming quickly—a glance of farewell, closing eyes, and—rest. But for hours and hours the struggle had gone on, a fight for breath that all the ward could hear. And he had not closed his eyes at all. They were turned up, and staring.

The Probationer had suffered horribly, and at last she had gone behind the screen and folded her hands and closed her eyes, and said very low:

"Dear God—please take him quickly."

He had stopped breathing almost immediately. But that may have been a coincidence.

However, she was not writing that home. Between gasps she was telling the humours of visiting day in the ward, and of how kind every one was to her, which, if not entirely true, was not entirely untrue. They were kind enough when they had time to be, or when they remembered her. Only they did not always remember her.

She ended by saying that she was quite sure they meant to accept her when her three months was up. It was frightfully necessary that she be accepted.

She sent messages to all the little town, which had seen her off almost en masse. And she added that the probationers received the regular first-year allowance of eight dollars a month, and she could make it do nicely—which was quite true, unless she kept on breaking thermometers when she shook them down.

At the end she sent her love to everybody, including even worthless Johnny Fraser, who cut the grass and scrubbed the porches; and, of course, to Doctor Willie. He was called Doctor Willie because his father, who had taken him into partnership long ago, was Doctor Will. It never had seemed odd, although Doctor Willie was now sixty-five, and a saintly soul.

Curiously enough, her letter was dated April first. Under that very date, and about that time of the day, a health officer in a near-by borough was making an entry regarding certain coloured gentlemen shipped north from Louisiana to work on a railroad. Opposite the name of one Augustus Baird he put a cross. This indicated that Augustus Baird had not been vaccinated.

By the sixth of April "Twenty-two" had progressed from splints to a plaster cast, and was being most awfully bored. Jane Brown had not returned, and there was a sort of relentless maturity about the nurses who looked after him that annoyed him.

Lying there, he had a good deal of time to study them, and somehow his recollection of the girl with the hunting-case watch did not seem to fit her in with these kindly and efficient women. He could not, for instance, imagine her patronising the Senior Surgical Interne in a deferential but unmistakable manner, or good-naturedly bullying the First Assistant, who was a nervous person in shoes too small for her, as to their days off duty.

Twenty-two began to learn things about the hospital. For instance, the day nurse, while changing his pillow slips, would observe that Nineteen was going to be operated on that day, and close her lips over further information. But when the afternoon relief, while giving him his toothbrush after lunch, said there was a most interesting gall-stone case in nineteen, and the night nurse, in reply to a direct question, told Nineteen's name, but nothing else, Twenty-two had a fair working knowledge of the day's events.

He seemed to learn about everything but Jane Brown. He knew when a new baby came, and was even given a glimpse of one, showing, he considered, about the colour and general contour of a maraschino cherry. And he learned soon that the god of the hospital is the Staff, although worship did not blind the nurses to their weaknesses. Thus the older men, who had been trained before the day of asepsis and modern methods, were revered but carefully watched. They would get out of scrubbing their hands whenever they could, and they hated their beards tied up with gauze. The nurses, keen, competent and kindly, but shrewd, too, looked after these elderly recalcitrants; loved a few, hated some, and presented to the world unbroken ranks for their defence.

Twenty-two learned also the story of the First Assistant, who was in love with one of the Staff, who was married, and did not care for her anyhow. So she wore tight shoes, and was always beautifully waved, and read Browning.

She had a way of coming in and saying brightly, as if to reassure herself:

"Good morning, Twenty-two. Well, God is still in His heaven, and all's well with the world."

Twenty-two got to feeling awfully uncomfortable about her. She used to bring him flowers and sit down a moment to rest her feet, which generally stung. And she would stop in the middle of a sentence and look into space, but always with a determined smile.

He felt awfully uncomfortable. She was so neat and so efficient—and so tragic. He tried to imagine being hopelessly in love, and trying to live on husks of Browning. Not even Mrs. Browning.

The mind is a curious thing. Suddenly, from thinking of Mrs. Browning, he thought of N. Jane Brown. Of course not by that ridiculous name. He had learned that she was stationed on that floor. And in the same flash he saw the Senior Surgical Interne swanking about in white ducks and just the object for a probationer to fall in love with. He lay there, and pulled the beginning of the new moustache, and reflected. The First Assistant was pinning a spray of hyacinth in her cap.

"Look here," he said. "Why can't I be put in a wheeled chair and get about? One that I can manipulate myself," he added craftily.

She demurred. Indeed, everybody demurred when he put it up to them. But he had gone through the world to the age of twenty-four, getting his own way about ninety-seven per cent. of the time. He got it this time, consisting of a new cast, which he named Elizabeth, and a roller-chair, and he spent a full day learning how to steer himself around.

Then, on the afternoon of the third day, rolling back toward the elevator and the terra incognita which lay beyond, he saw a sign. He stared at it blankly, because it interfered considerably with a plan he had in mind. The sign was of tin, and it said:

"No private patients allowed beyond here."

Twenty-two sat in his chair and stared at it. The plaster cast stretched out in front of him, and was covered by a grey blanket. With the exception of the trifling formality of trousers, he was well dressed in a sack coat, a shirt, waistcoat, and a sort of college-boy collar and tie, which one of the orderlies had purchased for him. His other things were in that extremely expensive English car which the city was storing.

The plain truth is that Twenty-two was looking for Jane Brown. Since she had not come to him, he must go to her. He particularly wanted to set her right as to Mabel. And he felt, too, that that trick about respirations had not been entirely fair.

He was, of course, not in the slightest degree in love with her. He had only seen her once, and then he had had a broken leg and a quarter grain of morphia and a burned moustache and no eyebrows left to speak of.

But there was the sign. It was hung to a nail beside the elevator shaft. And far beyond, down the corridor, was somebody in a blue dress and no cap. It might be anybody, but again— —

Twenty-two looked around. The elevator had just gone down at its usual rate of a mile every two hours. In the convalescent parlour, where private patients en negligée complained about the hospital food, the nurse in charge was making a new cap. Over all the hospital brooded an after-luncheon peace.

Twenty-two wheeled up under the sign and considered his average of ninety-seven per cent. Followed in sequence these events: (a) Twenty-two wheeled back to the parlour, where old Mr. Simond's cane leaned against a table, and, while engaging that gentleman in conversation, possessed himself of the cane. (b) Wheeled back to the elevator. (c) Drew cane from beneath blanket. (d) Unhooked sign with cane and concealed both under blanket. (e) Worked his way back along the forbidden territory, past I and J until he came to H ward.

Jane Brown was in H ward.

She was alone, and looking very professional. There is nothing quite so professional as a new nurse. She had, indeed, reached a point where, if she took a pulse three times, she got somewhat similar results. There had been a time when they had run something like this: $56-80-120--$

Jane Brown was taking pulses. It was a visiting day, and all the beds had fresh white spreads, tucked in neatly at the foot. In the exact middle of the centre table with its red cloth, was a vase of yellow tulips. The sun came in and turned them to golden flame.

Jane Brown was on duty alone and taking pulses with one eye while she watched the visitors with the other. She did the watching better than she did the pulses. For instance, she was distinctly aware that Stanislas Krzykolski's wife, in the bed next the end, had just slid a half-dozen greasy cakes, sprinkled with sugar, under his pillow. She knew, however, that not only grease but love was in those cakes, and she did not intend to confiscate them until after Mrs. Krzykolski had gone.

More visitors came. Shuffling and self-conscious mill-workers, walking on their toes; draggled women; a Chinese boy; a girl with a rouged face and a too confident manner. A hum of conversation hung over the long room. The sunlight came in and turned to glory, not only the tulips and the red tablecloth, but also the brass basins, the fireplace fender, and the Probationer's hair.

Twenty-two sat unnoticed in the doorway. A young girl, very lame, with a mandolin, had just entered the ward. In the little stir of her arrival, Twenty-two had time to see that Jane Brown was worth even all the trouble he had taken, and more. Really, to see Jane Brown properly, she should have always been seen in the sun. She was that sort.

The lame girl sat down in the centre of the ward, and the buzz died away. She was not pretty, and she was very nervous. Twenty-two frowned a trifle.

"Poor devils," he said to himself. But Jane Brown put away her hunting-case watch, and the lame girl swept the ward with soft eyes that had in them a pity that was almost a benediction.

Then she sang. Her voice was like her eyes, very sweet and rather frightened, but tender. And suddenly something a little hard and selfish in Twenty-two began to be horribly ashamed of itself. And, for no earthly reason in the world, he began to feel like a cumberer of the earth. Before she had finished the first song, he was thinking that perhaps when he was getting about again, he might run over to France for a few months in the ambulance service. A fellow really ought to do his bit.

At just about that point Jane Brown turned and saw him. And although he had run all these risks to get to her, and even then had an extremely cold tin sign lying on his knee under the blanket, at first she did not know him. The shock of this was almost too much for him. In all sorts of places people were glad to see him, especially women. He was astonished, but it was good for him.

She recognised him almost immediately, however, and flushed a little, because she knew he had no business there. She was awfully bound up with rules.

"I came back on purpose to see you," said Twenty-two, when at last the lame girl had limped away. "Because, that day I came in and you looked after me, you know, I—must have talked a lot of nonsense."

"Morphia makes some people talk," she said. It was said in an exact copy of the ward nurse's voice, a frightfully professional and impersonal tone.

"But," said Twenty-two, stirring uneasily, "I said a lot that wasn't true. You may have forgotten, but I haven't. Now that about a girl named Mabel, for instance——"

He stirred again, because, after all, what did it matter what he had said? She was gazing over the ward. She was not interested in him. She had almost forgotten him. And as he stirred Mr. Simond's cane fell out. It was immediately followed by the tin sign, which only gradually subsided, face up, on the bare floor, in a slowly diminishing series of crashes.

Jane Brown stooped and picked them both up and placed them on his lap. Then, very stern, she marched out of the ward into the corridor, and there subsided into quiet hysterics of mirth. Twenty-two, who hated to be laughed at, followed her in the chair, looking extremely annoyed.

"What else was I to do?" he demanded, after a time. "Of course, if you report it, I'm gone."

"What do you intend to do with it now?" she asked. All her professional manner had gone, and she looked alarmingly young.

"If I put it back, I'll only have to steal it again. Because I am absolutely bored to death in that room of mine. I have played a thousand games of solitaire."

The Probationer looked around. There was no one in sight.

"I should think," she suggested, "that if you slipped it behind that radiator, no one would ever know about it."

Fortunately, the ambulance gong set up a clamour below the window just then, and no one heard one of the hospital's most cherished rules going, as one may say, into the discard.

The Probationer leaned her nose against the window and looked down. A coloured man was being carried in on a stretcher. Although she did not know it—indeed, never did know it—the coloured gentleman in question was one Augustus Baird.

Soon afterward Twenty-two squeaked—his chair needed oiling—squeaked back to his lonely room and took stock. He found that he was rid of Mabel, but was still a reporter, hurt in doing his duty. He had let this go because he saw that duty was a sort of fetish with the Probationer. And since just now she liked him for what she thought he was, why not wait to tell her until she liked him for himself?

He hoped she was going to like him, because she was going to see him a lot. Also, he liked her even better than he had remembered that he did. She had a sort of thoroughbred look that he liked. And he liked the way her hair was soft and straight and shiny. And he liked the way she was all business and no nonsense. And the way she counted pulses, with her lips moving and a little frown between her eyebrows. And he liked her for being herself—which is, after all, the reason why most men like the women they like, and extremely reasonable.

The First Assistant loaned him Browning that afternoon, and he read "Pippa Passes." He thought Pippa must have looked like the Probationer.

The Head was a bit querulous that evening. The Heads of Training Schools get that way now and then, although they generally reveal it only to the First Assistant. They have to do so many irreconcilable things, such as keeping down expenses while keeping up requisitions, and remembering the different sorts of sutures the Staff likes, and receiving the Ladies' Committee, and conducting prayers and lectures, and knowing by a swift survey of a ward that the stands have been carbolised and all the toe-nails cut. Because it is amazing the way toe-nails grow in bed.

The Head would probably never have come out flatly, but she had a wretched cold, and the First Assistant was giving her a mustard footbath, which was very hot. The Head sat up with a blanket over her shoulders, and read lists while her feet took on the blush of ripe apples. And at last she said:

"How is that Probationer with the ridiculous name getting along?"

The First Assistant poured in more hot water.

"N. Jane?" she asked. "Well, she's a nice little thing, and she seems willing. But, of course——"

The Head groaned.

"Nineteen!" she said. "And no character at all. I detest fluttery people. She flutters the moment I go into the ward."

The First Assistant sat back and felt of her cap, which was of starched tulle and was softening a bit from the steam. She felt a thrill of pity for the Probationer. She, too, had once felt fluttery when the Head came in.

"She is very anxious to stay," she observed. "She works hard, too. I——"

"She has no personality, no decision," said the Head, and sneezed twice. She was really very wretched, and so she was unfair. "She is pretty and sweet. But I cannot run my training school on prettiness and sweetness. Has Doctor Harvard come in yet?"

"I—I think not," said the First Assistant. She looked up quickly, but the Head was squeezing a lemon in a cup of hot water beside her.

Now, while the Head was having a footbath, and Twenty-two was having a stock-taking, and Augustus Baird was having his symptoms recorded, Jane Brown was having a shock.

She heard an unmistakable shuffling of feet in the corridor.

Sounds take on much significance in a hospital, and probationers study them, especially footsteps. It gives them a moment sometimes to think what to do next.

Internes, for instance, frequently wear rubber soles on their white shoes and have a way of slipping up on one. And the engineer goes on a half run, generally accompanied by the clanking of a tool or two. And the elevator man runs, too, because generally the bell is ringing. And ward patients shuffle about in carpet slippers, and the pharmacy clerk has a brisk young step, inclined to be jaunty.

But it is the Staff which is always unmistakable. It comes along the corridor deliberately, inexorably. It plants its feet firmly and with authority. It moves with the inevitability of fate, with the pride of royalty, with the ease of the best made-to-order boots. The ring of a Staff member's heel on a hospital corridor is the most authoritative sound on earth. He may be the gentlest soul in the world, but he will tread like royalty.

But this was not Staff. Jane Brown knew this sound, and it filled her with terror. It was the scuffling of four pairs of feet, carefully instructed not to keep step. It meant, in other words, a stretcher. But perhaps it was not coming to her. Ah, but it was!

Panic seized Jane Brown. She knew there were certain things to do, but they went out of her mind like a cat out of a cellar window. However, the ward was watching. It had itself, generally speaking, come in feet first. It knew the procedure. So, instructed by low voices from the beds around,

Jane Brown feverishly tore the spread off the emergency bed and drew it somewhat apart from its fellows. Then she stood back and waited.

Came in four officers from the police patrol. Came in the Senior Surgical Interne. Came two convalescents from the next ward to stare in at the door. Came the stretcher, containing a quiet figure under a grey blanket.

Twenty-two, at that exact moment, was putting a queen on a ten spot and pretending there is nothing wrong about cheating oneself.

In a very short time the quiet figure was on the bed, and the Senior Surgical Interne was writing in the order book: "Prepare for operation."

Jane Brown read it over his shoulder, which is not etiquette.

"But—I can't," she quavered. "I don't know how. I won't touch him. He's—he's bloody!"

Then she took another look at the bed and she saw—Johnny Fraser.

Now Johnny had, in his small way, played a part in the Probationer's life, such as occasionally scrubbing porches or borrowing a half dollar or being suspected of stealing the eggs from the henhouse. But that Johnny Fraser had been a wicked, smiling imp, much given to sitting in the sun.

Here lay another Johnny Fraser, a quiet one, who might never again feel the warm earth through his worthless clothes on his worthless young body. A Johnny of closed eyes and slow, noisy breathing.

"Why, Johnny!" said the Probationer, in a strangled voice.

The Senior Surgical Interne was interested.

"Know him?" he said.

"He is a boy from home." She was still staring at this quiet, un-impudent figure.

The Senior Surgical Interne eyed her with an eye that was only partially professional. Then he went to the medicine closet and poured a bit of aromatic ammonia into a glass.

"Sit down and drink this," he said, in a very masculine voice. He liked to feel that he could do something for her. Indeed, there was something almost proprietary in the way he took her pulse.

Some time after the early hospital supper that evening Twenty-two, having oiled his chair with some olive oil from his tray, made a clandestine trip through the twilight of the corridor back of the elevator shaft. To avoid scandal he pretended interest in other wards, but he gravitated, as a needle to the pole, to H. And there he found the Probationer, looking rather strained, and mothering a quiet figure on a bed.

He was a trifle puzzled at her distress, for she made no secret of Johnny's status in the community. What he did not grasp was that Johnny Fraser was a link between this new and rather terrible world of the hospital and home. It was not Johnny alone, it was Johnny scrubbing a home porch and doing it badly, it was Johnny in her father's old clothes, it was Johnny fishing for catfish in the creek, or lending his pole to one of the little brothers whose pictures were on her table in the dormitory.

Twenty-two felt a certain depression. He reflected rather grimly that he had been ten days missing and that no one had apparently given a hang whether he turned up or not.

"Is he going to live?" he inquired. He could see that the ward nurse had an eye on him, and was preparing for retreat.

"O yes," said Jane Brown. "I think so now. The interne says they have had a message from Doctor Willie. He is coming." There was a beautiful confidence in her tone.

Things moved very fast with the Probationer for the next twenty-four hours. Doctor Willie came, looking weary but smiling benevolently. Jane

Brown met him in a corridor and kissed him, as, indeed, she had been in the habit of doing since her babyhood.

"Where is the young rascal?" said Doctor Willie. "Up to his old tricks, Nellie, and struck by a train." He put a hand under her chin, which is never done to the members of the training school in a hospital, and searched her face with his kind old eyes. "Well, how does it go, Nellie?"

Jane Brown swallowed hard.

"All right," she managed. "They want to operate, Doctor Willie."

"Tut!" he said. "Always in a hurry, these hospitals. We'll wait a while, I think."

"Is everybody well at home?"

It had come to her, you see, what comes to every nurse once in her training—the thinness of the veil, the terror of calamity, the fear of death.

"All well. And——" he glanced around. Only the Senior Surgical Interne was in sight, and he was out of hearing. "Look here, Nellie," he said, "I've got a dozen fresh eggs for you in my satchel. Your mother sent them."

She nearly lost her professional manner again then. But she only asked him to warn the boys about automobiles and riding on the backs of wagons.

Had any one said Twenty-two to her, she would not have known what was meant. Not just then, anyhow.

In the doctors' room that night the Senior Surgical Interne lighted a cigarette and telephoned to the operating room.

"That trephining's off," he said, briefly.

Then he fell to conversation with the Senior Medical, who was rather worried about a case listed on the books as Augustus Baird, coloured.

Twenty-two did not sleep very well that night. He needed exercise, he felt. But there was something else. Miss Brown had been just a shade too ready to accept his explanation about Mabel, he felt, so ready that he feared she had been more polite than sincere. Probably she still believed there was a Mabel. Not that it mattered, except that he hated to make a fool of himself. He roused once in the night and was quite sure he heard her voice down the corridor. He knew this must be wrong, because they would not make her work all day and all night, too.

But, as it happened, it was Jane Brown. The hospital provided plenty of sleeping time, but now and then there was a slip-up and somebody paid. There had been a night operation, following on a busy day, and the operating-room nurses needed help. Out of a sound sleep the night Assistant had summoned Jane Brown to clean instruments.

At five o'clock that morning she was still sitting on a stool beside a glass table, polishing instruments which made her shiver. All around were things that were spattered with blood. But she looked anything but fluttery. She was a very grim and determined young person just then, and professional beyond belief. The other things, like washing window-sills and cutting toe-nails, had had no significance. But here she was at last on the edge of mercy. Some one who might have died had lived that night because of this room, and these instruments, and willing hands.

She hoped she would always have willing hands.

She looked very pale at breakfast the next morning, and rather older. Also she had a new note of authority in her voice when she telephoned the kitchen and demanded H ward's soft-boiled eggs. She washed window-sills that morning again, but no longer was there rebellion in her soul. She was seeing suddenly how the hospital required all these menial services, which were not menial at all but only preparation; that there were little tasks and big ones, and one graduated from the one to the other.

She took some flowers from the ward bouquet and put them beside Johnny's bed—Johnny, who was still lying quiet, with closed eyes.

The Senior Surgical Interne did a dressing in the ward that morning. He had been in to see Augustus Baird, and he felt uneasy. He vented it on Tony, the Italian, with a stiletto thrust in his neck, by jerking at the adhesive. Tony wailed, and Jane Brown, who was the "dirty" nurse—which does not mean what it appears to mean, but is the person who receives the soiled dressings—Jane Brown gritted her teeth.

"Keep quiet," said the S.S.I., who was a good fellow, but had never been stabbed in the neck for running away with somebody else's wife.

"Eet hurt," said Tony. "Ow."

Jane Brown turned very pink.

"Why don't you let me cut it off properly?" she said, in a strangled tone.

The total result of this was that Jane Brown was reprimanded by the First Assistant, and learned some things about ethics.

"But," she protested, "it was both stupid and cruel. And if I know I am right——"

"How are you to know you are right?" demanded the First Assistant, crossly. Her feet were stinging. "'A little knowledge is a dangerous thing.'" This was a favorite quotation of hers, although not Browning. "Nurses in hospitals are there to carry out the doctor's orders. Not to think or to say what they think unless they are asked. To be intelligent, but——"

"But not too intelligent!" said the Probationer. "I see."

This was duly reported to the Head, who observed that it was merely what she had expected and extremely pert. Her cold was hardly any better.

It was taking the Probationer quite a time to realise her own total lack of significance in all this. She had been accustomed to men who rose when a woman entered a room and remained standing as long as she stood. And now she was in a new world, where she had to rise and remain standing while a cocky youth in ducks, just out of medical college, sauntered in with his hands in his pockets and took a boutonnière from the ward bouquet.

It was probably extremely good for her.

She was frightfully tired that day, and toward evening the little glow of service began to fade. There seemed to be nothing to do for Johnny but to wait. Doctor Willie had seemed to think that nature would clear matters up there, and had requested no operation. She smoothed beds and carried cups of water and broke another thermometer. And she put the eggs from home in the ward pantry and made egg-nogs of them for Stanislas Krzykolski, who was unaccountably upset as to stomach.

She had entirely forgotten Twenty-two. He had stayed away all that day, in a sort of faint hope that she would miss him. But she had not. She was feeling rather worried, to tell the truth. For a Staff surgeon going through the ward, had stopped by Johnny's bed and examined the pupils of his eyes, and had then exchanged a glance with the Senior Surgical Interne that had perplexed her.

In the chapel at prayers that evening all around her the nurses sat and rested, their tired hands folded in their laps. They talked a little among themselves, but it was only a buzzing that reached the Probationer faintly. Some one near was talking about something that was missing.

"Gone?" she said. "Of course it is gone. The bath-room man reported it to me and I went and looked."

"But who in the world would take it?"

"My dear," said the first speaker, "who does take things in a hospital, anyhow? Only — a tin sign!"

It was then that the Head came in. She swept in; her grey gown, her grey hair gave her a majesty that filled the Probationer with awe. Behind her came the First Assistant with the prayer-book and hymnal. The Head believed in form.

Jane Brown offered up a little prayer that night for Johnny Fraser, and another little one without words, that Doctor Willie was right. She sat and rested her weary young body, and remembered how Doctor Willie was loved and respected, and the years he had cared for the whole countryside. And the peace of the quiet room, with the Easter lilies on the tiny altar, brought rest to her.

It was when prayers were over that the Head made her announcement. She rose and looked over the shadowy room, where among the rows of white caps only the Probationer's head was uncovered, and she said:

"I have an announcement to make to the training school. One which I regret, and which will mean a certain amount of hardship and deprivation.

"A case of contagion has been discovered in one of the wards, and it has been considered necessary to quarantine the hospital. The doors were closed at seven-thirty this evening."

II

Considering that he could not get out anyhow, Twenty-two took the news of the quarantine calmly. He reflected that, if he was shut in, Jane Brown was shut in also. He had a wicked hope, at the beginning, that the Senior Surgical Interne had been shut out, but at nine o'clock that evening that young gentleman showed up at the door of his room, said "Cheer-o," came in, helped himself to a cigarette, gave a professional glance at Twenty-two's toes, which were all that was un-plastered of the leg, and departing threw back over his shoulder his sole conversational effort:

"Hell of a mess, isn't it?"

Twenty-two took up again gloomily the book he was reading, which was on Diseases of the Horse, from the hospital library. He was in the midst of Glanders.

He had, during most of that day, been making up his mind to let his family know where he was. He did not think they cared, particularly. He had no illusions about that. But there was something about Jane Brown which made him feel like doing the decent thing. It annoyed him frightfully, but there it was. She was so eminently the sort of person who believed in doing the decent thing.

So, about seven o'clock, he had sent the orderly out for stamps and paper. He imagined that Jane Brown would not think writing home on hospital stationery a good way to break bad news. But the orderly had stopped for a chat at the engine house, and had ended by playing a game of dominoes. When, at ten o'clock, he had returned to the hospital entrance, the richer by a quarter and a glass of beer, he had found a strange policeman on the hospital steps, and the doors locked.

The quarantine was on.

Now there are different sorts of quarantines. There is the sort where a trained nurse and the patient are shut up in a room and bath, and the family only opens the door and peers in. And there is the sort where the front door has a placard on it, and the family goes in and out the back way, and takes a street-car to the office, the same as usual. And there is the hospital quarantine, which is the real thing, because hospitals are expected to do things thoroughly.

So our hospital was closed up as tight as a jar of preserves. There were policemen at all the doors, quite suddenly. They locked the doors and put the keys in their pockets, and from that time on they opened them only to pass things in, such as newspapers or milk or groceries or the braver members of the Staff. But not to let anything out—except the Staff. Supposedly Staffs do not carry germs.

And, indeed, even the Staff was not keen about entering. It thought of a lot of things it ought to do about visiting time, and prescribed considerably over the telephone.

At first there was a great deal of confusion, because quite a number of people had been out on various errands when it happened. And they came back, and protested to the office that they had only their uniforms on under their coats, and three dollars; or their slippers and no hats. Or that they would sue the city. One or two of them got quite desperate and tried to crawl up the fire-escape, but failed.

This is of interest chiefly because it profoundly affected Jane Brown. Miss McAdoo, her ward nurse, had debated whether to wash her hair that evening, or to take a walk. She had decided on the walk, and was therefore shut out, along with the Junior Medical, the kitchen cat, the Superintendent's mother-in-law and six other nurses.

The next morning the First Assistant gave Jane Brown charge of H ward.

"It's very irregular," she said. "I don't exactly know—you have only one bad case, haven't you?"

"Only Johnny."

The First Assistant absent-mindedly ran a finger over the top of a table, and examined it for dust.

"Of course," she said, "it's a great chance for you. Show that you can handle this ward, and you are practically safe."

Jane Brown drew a long breath and stood up very straight. Then she ran her eye over the ward. There was something vaguely reminiscent of Miss McAdoo in her glance.

Twenty-two made three brief excursions back along the corridor that first day of the quarantine. But Jane Brown was extremely professional and very busy. There was an air of discipline over the ward. Let a man but so much as turn over in bed and show an inch of blanket, and she pounced on the bed and reduced it to the most horrible neatness. All the beds looked as if they had been made up with a carpenter's square.

On the third trip, however, Jane Brown was writing at the table. Twenty-two wheeled himself into the doorway and eyed her with disapproval.

"What do you mean by sitting down?" he demanded sarcastically. "Don't you know that now you are in charge you ought to keep moving?"

To which she replied, absently:

"Three buttered toasts, two dry toasts, six soft boiled eggs, and twelve soups." She was working on the diet slips.

Then she smiled at him. They were quite old friends already. It is curious about love and friendship and all those kindred emotions. They do not grow nearly so fast when people are together as when they are apart. It is an actual fact that the growth of many an intimacy is checked by meetings. Because when people are apart it is what they are that counts, and when they are together it is what they do and say and look like. Many a beautiful affair has been ruined because, just as it was going along well, the principals met again.

However, all this merely means that Twenty-two and Jane Brown were infinitely closer friends than four or five meetings really indicates.

The ward was very quiet on this late afternoon call of his save for Johnny's heavy breathing. There is a quiet hour in a hospital, between afternoon temperatures and the ringing of the bell which means that the suppers for the wards are on their way — a quiet hour when over the long rows of beds broods the peace of the ending day.

It is a melancholy hour, too, because from the streets comes faintly the echo of feet hurrying home, the eager trot of a horse bound stableward. To those in the eddy that is the ward comes at this time a certain heaviness of spirit. Poor thing though home may have been, they long for it.

In H ward that late afternoon there was a wave of homesickness in the air, and on the part of those men who were up and about, who shuffled up and down the ward in flapping carpet slippers, an inclination to mutiny.

"How did they take it?" Twenty-two inquired. She puckered her eyebrows.

"They don't like it," she confessed. "Some of them were about ready to go home and it — Tony!" she called sharply.

For Tony, who had been cunningly standing by the window leading to a fire-escape, had flung the window up and was giving unmistakable signs of climbing out and returning to the other man's wife.

"Tony!" she called, and ran. Tony scrambled up on the sill. A sort of titter ran over the ward and Tony, now on the platform outside, waved a derisive hand through the window.

"Good-bye, mees!" he said, and — disappeared.

It was not a very dramatic thing, after all. It is chiefly significant for its effect on Twenty-two, who was obliged to sit frozen with horror and cursing his broken leg, while Jane Brown raced a brown little Italian down the fire-escape and caught him at the foot of it. Tony took a look around.

The courtyard gates were closed and a policeman sat outside on a camp-stool reading the newspaper. Tony smiled sheepishly and surrendered.

Some seconds later Tony and Jane Brown appeared on the platform outside. Jane Brown had Tony by the ear, and she stopped long enough outside to exchange the ear for his shoulder, by which she shook him, vigorously.

Twenty-two turned his chair around and wheeled himself back to his room. He was filled with a cold rage—because she might have fallen on the fire-escape and been killed; because he had not been able to help her; because she was there, looking after the derelicts of life, when the world was beautiful outside, and she was young; because to her he was just Twenty-two and nothing more.

He had seen her exactly six times.

Jane Brown gave the ward a little talk that night before the night nurse reported. She stood in the centre of the long room, beside the tulips, and said that she was going to be alone there, and that she would have to put the situation up to their sense of honour. If they tried to escape, they would hurt her. Also they would surely be caught and brought back. And, because she believed in a combination of faith and deeds, she took three nails and the linen-room flatiron, and nailed shut the window onto the fire-escape.

After that, she brushed crumbs out of the beds with a whiskbroom and rubbed a few backs with alcohol, and smoothed the counterpanes, and hung over Johnny's unconscious figure for a little while, giving motherly pats to his flat pillow and worrying considerably because there was so little about him to remind her of the Johnny she knew at home.

After that she sat down and made up her records for the night nurse. The ward understood, and was perfectly good, trying hard not to muss its pillows or wrinkle the covers. And struggling, too, with a new idea. They were prisoners. No more release cards would brighten the days. For an indefinite period the old Frenchman would moan at night, and Bader the German would snore, and the Chinaman would cough. Indefinitely they would eat soft-boiled eggs and rice and beef-tea and cornstarch.

The ward felt extremely low in its mind.

That night the Senior Surgical Interne went in to play cribbage with Twenty-two, and received a lecture on leaving a young girl alone in H with a lot of desperate men. They both grew rather heated over the discussion and forgot to play cribbage at all. Twenty-two lay awake half the night, because he had seen clearly that the Senior Surgical Interne was interested in Jane Brown also, and would probably loaf around H most of the time since there would be no new cases now. It was a crowning humiliation to have the night nurse apply to the Senior Surgical Interne for a sleeping powder for him!

Toward morning he remembered that he had promised to write out from memory one of the Sonnets from the Portuguese for the First Assistant, and he turned on the light and jotted down two lines of it. He wrote:

"For we two look two ways, and cannot shine

With the same sunlight on our brow and hair." —

And then sat up in bed for half an hour looking at it because he was so awfully afraid it was true of Jane Brown and himself. Not, of course, that he wanted to shine at all. It was the looking two ways that hurt.

The next evening the nurses took their airing on the roof, which was a sooty place with a parapet, and in the courtyard, which was an equally sooty place with a wispy fountain. And because the whole situation was new, they formed in little groups on the wooden benches and sang, hands folded on white aprons, heads lifted, eyes upturned to where, above the dimly lighted windows, the stars peered palely through the smoke.

The S.S.I. sauntered out. He had thought he saw the Probationer from his window, and in the new relaxation of discipline he saw a chance to join her. But the figure he had thought he recognised proved to be some one else, and he fell to wandering alone up and down the courtyard.

He was trying to work out this problem: would the advantage of marrying early and thus being considered eligible for certain cases, offset the disadvantage of the extra expense?

He decided to marry early and hang the expense.

The days went by, three, then four, and a little line of tension deepened around Jane Brown's mouth. Perhaps it has not been mentioned that she had a fighting nose, short and straight, and a wistful mouth. For Johnny Fraser was still lying in a stupor.

Jane Brown felt that something was wrong. Doctor Willie came in once or twice, making the long trip without complaint and without hope of payment. All his busy life he had worked for the sake of work, and not for reward. He called her "Nellie," to the delight of the ward, which began to love him, and he spent a long hour each time by Johnny's bed. But the Probationer was quick to realise that the Senior Surgical Interne disapproved of him.

That young man had developed a tendency to wander into H at odd hours, and sit on the edge of a table, leaving Jane Brown divided between proper respect for an interne and fury over the wrinkling of her table covers. It was during one of these visits that she spoke of Doctor Willie.

"Because he is a country practitioner," she said, "you—you patronise him."

"Not at all," said the Senior Surgical Interne. "Personally I like him immensely."

"Personally!"

The Senior Surgical Interne waved a hand toward Johnny's bed.

"Look there," he said. "You don't think that chap's getting any better, do you?"

"If," said Jane Brown, with suspicious quiet, "if you think you know more than a man who has practised for forty years, and saved more people than you ever saw, why don't you tell him so?"

There is really no defence for this conversation. Discourse between a probationer and an interne is supposed to be limited to yea, yea, and nay, nay. But the circumstances were unusual.

"Tell him!" exclaimed the Senior Surgical Interne, "and be called before the Executive Committee and fired! Dear girl, I am inexpressibly flattered, but the voice of an interne in a hospital is the voice of one crying in the wilderness."

Twenty-two, who was out on crutches that day for the first time, and was looking very big and extremely awkward, Twenty-two looked back from the elevator shaft and scowled. He seemed always to see a flash of white duck near the door of H ward.

To add to his chagrin, the Senior Surgical Interne clapped him on the back in congratulation a moment later, and nearly upset him. He had intended to go back to the ward and discuss a plan he had, but he was very morose those days and really not a companionable person. He stumped back to his room and resolutely went to bed.

There he lay for a long time looking at the ceiling, and saying, out of his misery, things not necessary to repeat.

So Twenty-two went to bed and sulked, refusing supper, and having the word "Vicious" marked on his record by the nurse, who hoped he would see it some time. And Jane Brown went and sat beside a strangely silent Johnny, and worried. And the Senior Surgical Interne went down to the pharmacy and thereby altered a number of things.

The pharmacy clerk had been shaving—his own bedroom was dark—and he saw the Senior Surgical Interne in the little mirror hung on the window frame.

"Hello," he said, over the soap. "Shut the door."

The Senior Surgical Interne shut the door, and then sniffed. "Smells like a bar-room," he commented.

The pharmacy clerk shaved the left angle of his jaw, and then turned around.

"Little experiment of mine," he explained. "Simple syrup, grain alcohol, a dash of cochineal for colouring, and some flavouring extract. It's an imitation cordial. Try it."

The Senior Surgical Interne was not a drinker, but he was willing to try anything once. So he secured a two-ounce medicine glass, and filled it.

"Looks nice," he commented, and tasted it. "It's not bad."

"Not bad!" said the pharmacy clerk. "You'd pay four dollars a bottle for that stuff in a hotel. Actual cost here, about forty cents."

The Senior Surgical Interne sat down and stretched out his legs. He had the glass in his hand.

"It's rather sweet," he said. "But it looks pretty." He took another sip.

After he had finished it, he got to thinking things over. He felt about seven feet tall and very important, and not at all like a voice crying in the wilderness. He had a strong inclination to go into the Superintendent's office and tell him where he went wrong in running the institution—which he restrained. And another to go up to H and tell Jane Brown the truth about Johnny Fraser—which he yielded to.

On the way up he gave the elevator man a cigar.

He was very explicit with Jane Brown.

"Your man's wrong, that's all there is about it," he said. "I can't say anything and you can't. But he's wrong. That's an operative case. The Staff knows it."

"Then, why doesn't the Staff do it?"

The Senior Surgical Interne was still feeling very tall. He looked down at her from a great distance.

"Because, dear child," he said, "it's your man's case. You ought to know enough about professional ethics for that."

He went away, then, and had a violent headache, which he blamed on confinement and lack of exercise. But he had sowed something in the Probationer's mind.

For she knew, suddenly, that he had been right. The Staff had meant that, then, when they looked at Johnny and shook their heads. The Staff knew, the hospital knew. Every one knew but Doctor Willie. But Doctor Willie had the case. Back in her little town Johnny's mother was looking to Doctor Willie, believing in him, hoping through him.

That night Twenty-two slept, and Jane Brown lay awake. And down in H ward Johnny Fraser had a bad spell at that hour toward dawn when the vitality is low, and men die. He did not die, however. But the night nurse recorded, "Pulse very thin and iregular," at four o'clock.

She, too, was not a famous speller.

During the next morning, while the ward rolled bandages, having carefully scrubbed its hands first, Jane Brown wrote records—she did it rather well now—and then arranged the pins in the ward pincushion. She made concentric circles of safety-pins outside and common pins inside, with a large H in the centre. But her mind was not on this artistic bit of creation. It was on Johnny Fraser.

She made up her mind to speak to Doctor Willie.

Twenty-two had got over his sulking or his jealousy, or whatever it was, and during the early hours, those hours when Johnny was hardly breathing, he had planned something. He thought that he did it to interest the patients and make them contented, but somewhere in the back of his mind he knew it was to see more of Jane Brown. He planned a concert in the chapel.

So that morning he took Elizabeth, the plaster cast, back to H ward, where Jane Brown was fixing the pincushion, and had a good minute of feasting his eyes on her while she was sucking a jabbed finger. She knew she should have dipped the finger in a solution, but habit is strong in most of us.

Twenty-two had a wild desire to offer to kiss the finger and make it well. This, however, was not habit. It was insanity. He recognised this himself, and felt more than a trifle worried about it, because he had been in love quite a number of times before, but he had never had this sort of feeling.

He put the concert up to her with a certain amount of anxiety. If she could sing, or play, or recite—although he hoped she would not recite—all would be well. But if she refused to take any part, he did not intend to have a concert. That was flat.

"I can play," she said, making a neat period after the H on the pincushion.

He was awfully relieved.

"Good," he said. "You know, I like the way you say that. It's so—well, it's so competent." He got out a notebook and wrote "Miss Brown, piano selections."

It was while he was writing that Jane Brown had a sort of mental picture—the shabby piano at home, kicked below by many childish feet, but mellow and sweet, like an old violin, and herself sitting practising, over and over, that part of Paderewski's Minuet where, as every one knows, the fingering is rather difficult, and outside the open window, leaning on his broom, worthless Johnny Fraser, staring in with friendly eyes and an extremely dirty face. To Twenty-two's unbounded amazement she flung down the cushion and made for the little ward linen room.

He found her there a moment later, her arms outstretched on the table and her face buried in them. Some one had been boiling a rubber tube and had let the pan go dry. Ever afterward Twenty-two was to associate the smell of burning rubber with Jane Brown, and with his first real knowledge that he was in love with her.

He stumped in after her and closed the door, and might have ruined everything then and there by taking her in his arms, crutch and all. But the smell of burning rubber is a singularly permeating one, and he was kept from one indiscretion by being discovered in another.

It was somewhat later that Jane Brown was reprimanded for being found in the linen room with a private patient. She made no excuse, but something a little defiant began to grow in her eyes. It was not that she loved her work less. She was learning, day by day, the endless sacrifices of this profession she had chosen, its unselfishness, its grinding hard work, the payment that may lie in a smile of gratitude, the agony of pain that cannot be relieved. She went through her days with hands held out for service, and at night, in the chapel, she whispered soundless little prayers to be accepted, and to be always gentle and kind. She did not want to become a machine. She knew, although she had no words for it, the difference between duty and service.

But—a little spirit of rebellion was growing in her breast. She did not understand about Johnny Fraser, for one thing. And the matter of the linen room hurt. There seemed to be too many rules.

Then, too, she began to learn that hospitals had limitations. Jane Brown's hospital had no social worker. Much as she loved the work, the part that the hospital could not do began to hurt her. Before the quarantine women with new babies had gone out, without an idea of where to spend the night. Ailing children had gone home to such places as she could see from the dormitory windows, where the work the hospital had begun could not be finished.

From the roof of the building at night she looked out over a city that terrified her. The call of a playing child in the street began to sound to her like the shriek of accident. The very grinding of the trolley cars, the smoke of the mills, began to mean the operating room. She thought a great deal, those days, about the little town she had come from, with its peace and quiet streets. The city seemed cruel. But now and then she learned that if cities are cruel, men are kind.

Thus, on the very day of the concert, the quarantine was broken for a few minutes. It was broken forcibly, and by an officer of the law. A little newsie, standing by a fire at the next corner, for the spring day was cold, had caught fire. The big corner man had seen it all. He stripped off his overcoat, rolled the boy in it, and ran to the hospital. Here he was confronted by a brother officer, who was forbidden to admit him. The corner man did the thing that seemed quickest. He laid the newsie on the ground, knocked out the quarantine officer in two blows, broke the glass of the door with a third, slipped a bolt, and then, his burden in his arms, stalked in.

It did not lessen the majesty of that entrance that he was crying all the time.

The Probationer pondered that story when she heard it. After all, laws were right and good, but there were higher things than laws. She went and stood by Johnny's bed for a long time, thinking.

In the meantime, unexpected talent for the concert had developed. The piano in the chapel proving out of order, the elevator man proved to have been a piano tuner. He tuned it with a bone forceps. Strange places, hospitals, into which drift men from every walk of life, to find a haven and peace within their quiet walls. Old Tony had sung, in his youth, in the opera at Milan. A pretty young nurse went around the corridors muttering bits of "Orphant Annie" to herself. The Senior Surgical Interne was to sing the "Rosary," and went about practising to himself. He came into H ward and sang it through for Jane Brown, with his heart in his clear young eyes. He sang about the hours he had spent with her being strings of pearls, and all that, but he was really asking her if she would be willing to begin life with him in a little house, where she would have to answer the door-bell and watch telephone calls while he was out.

Jane Brown felt something of this, too. For she said: "You sing it beautifully," although he had flatted at least three times.

He wrote his name on a medicine label and glued it to her hand. It looked alarmingly possessive.

Twenty-two presided at the concert that night. He was extravagantly funny, and the sort of creaking solemnity with which things began turned to uproarious laughter very soon.

Everything went off wonderfully. Tony started his selection too high, and was obliged to stop and begin over again. And the two Silversteins, from the children's ward, who were to dance a Highland fling together, had a violent quarrel at the last moment and had to be scratched. But everything else went well. The ambulance driver gave a bass solo, and kept a bar or two ahead of the accompaniment, dodging chords as he did wagons on the street, and fetching up with a sort of garrison finish much as he brought in the ambulance.

But the real musical event of the evening was Jane Brown's playing. She played Schubert without any notes, because she had been taught to play Schubert that way.

And when they called her back, she played little folk songs of the far places of Europe. Standing around the walls, in wheeled chairs, on crutches, pale with the hospital pallor, these aliens in their eddy listened and thrilled. Some of them wept, but they smiled also.

At the end she played the Minuet, with a sort of flaming look in her eyes that puzzled Twenty-two. He could not know that she was playing it to Johnny Fraser, lying with closed eyes in the ward upstairs. He did not realise that there was a passion of sacrifice throbbing behind the dignity of the music.

Doctor Willie had stayed over for the concert. He sat, beaming benevolently, in the front row, and toward the end he got up and told some stories. After all, it was Doctor Willie who was the real hit of the evening. The convalescents rocked with joy in their roller chairs. Crutches came down in loud applause. When he sat down he slipped a big hand over Jane Brown's and gave hers a hearty squeeze.

"How d'you like me as a parlour entertainer, Nellie?" he whispered.

She put her other hand over his. Somehow she could not speak.

The First Assistant called to the Probationer that night as she went past her door. Lights were out, so the First Assistant had a candle, and she was rubbing her feet with witch hazel.

"Come in," she called. "I have been looking for you. I have some news for you."

The exaltation of the concert had died away. Jane Brown, in the candle light, looked small and tired and very, very young.

"We have watched you carefully," said the First Assistant, who had her night garments on but had forgotten to take off her cap. "Although you are young, you have shown ability, and — you are to be accepted."

"Thank you, very much," replied Jane Brown, in a strangled tone.

"At first," said the First Assistant, "we were not sure. You were very young, and you had such odd ideas. You know that yourself now."

She leaned down and pressed a sore little toe with her forefinger. Then she sighed. The mention of Jane Brown's youth had hurt her, because she was no longer very young. And there were times when she was tired, when it seemed to her that only youth counted. She felt that way to-night.

When Jane Brown had gone on, she blew out her candle and went to bed, still in her cap.

Hospitals do not really sleep at night. The elevator man dozes in his cage, and the night watchman may nap in the engineer's room in the basement. But the night nurses are always making their sleepless rounds, and in the wards, dark and quiet, restless figures turn and sigh.

Before she went to bed that night, Jane Brown, by devious ways, slipped back to her ward. It looked strange to her, this cavernous place, filled with the unlovely noises of sleeping men. By the one low light near the doorway she went back to Johnny's bed, and sat down beside him. She felt that this was the place to think things out. In her room other things pressed in on her; the necessity of making good for the sake of those at home, her love of the work, and cowardice. But here she saw things right.

The night nurse found her there some time later, asleep, her hunting-case watch open on Johnny's bed and her fingers still on his quiet wrist. She made no report of it.

Twenty-two had another sleepless night written in on his record that night. He sat up and worried. He worried about the way the Senior Surgical Interne had sung to Jane Brown that night. And he worried about things he had done and shouldn't have, and things he should have done and hadn't. Mostly the first. At five in the morning he wrote a letter to his family telling them where he was, and that he had been vaccinated and that the letter would be fumigated. He also wrote a check for an artificial leg for the boy in the children's ward, and then went to bed and put himself to sleep by reciting the "Rosary" over and over. His last conscious thought was that the hours he had spent with a certain person would not make much of a string of pearls.

The Probationer went to Doctor Willie the next day. Some of the exuberance of the concert still bubbled in him, although he shook his head over Johnny's record.

"A little slow, Nellie," he said. "A little slow."

Jane Brown took a long breath.

"Doctor Willie," she said, "won't you have him operated on?"

He looked up at her over his spectacles.

"Operated on? What for?"

"Well, he's not getting any better," she managed desperately. "I'm—sometimes I think he'll die while we're waiting for him to get better."

He was surprised, but he was not angry.

"There's no fracture, child," he said gently. "If there is a clot there, nature is probably better at removing it than we are. The trouble with you," he said indulgently, "is that you have come here, where they operate first and regret afterward. Nature is the best surgeon, child."

She cast about her despairingly for some way to tell him the truth. But even when she spoke she knew she was foredoomed to failure.

"But—suppose the Staff thinks that he should be?"

Doctor Willie's kindly mouth set itself into grim lines.

"The Staff!" he said, and looked at her searchingly. Then his jaws set at an obstinate angle.

"Well, Nellie," he said, "I guess one opinion's as good as another in these cases. And I don't suppose they'll do any cutting and hacking without my consent." He looked at Johnny's unconscious figure. "He never amounted to much," he added, "but it's surprising the way money's been coming in to pay his board here. Your mother sent five dollars. A good lot of people are interested in him. I can't see myself going home and telling them he died on the operating table."

He patted her on the arm as he went out.

"Don't get an old head on those young shoulders yet, Nellie," he said as he was going. "Leave the worrying to me. I'm used to it."

She saw then that to him she was still a little girl. She probably would always be just a little girl to him. He did not take her seriously, and no one else would speak to him. She was quite despairing.

The ward loved Doctor Willie since the night before. It watched him out with affectionate eyes. Jane Brown watched him, too, his fine old head, the sturdy step that had brought healing and peace to a whole county. She had hurt him, she knew that. She ached at the thought of it. And she had done no good.

That afternoon Jane Brown broke another rule. She went to Twenty-two on her off duty, and caused a mild furore there. He had been drawing a sketch of her from memory, an extremely poor sketch, with one eye larger than the other. He hid it immediately, although she could not possibly have recognised it, and talked very fast to cover his excitement.

"Well, well!" he said. "I knew I was going to have some luck to-day. My right hand has been itching—or is that a sign of money?" Then he saw her face, and reduced his speech to normality, if not his heart.

"Come and sit down," he said. "And tell me about it."

But she would not sit down. She went to the window and looked out for a moment. It was from there she said:

"I have been accepted."

"Good." But he did not, apparently, think it such good news. He drew a long breath. "Well, I suppose your friends should be glad for you."

"I didn't come to talk about being accepted," she announced.

"I don't suppose, by any chance, you came to see how I am getting along?" he inquired humbly.

"I can see that."

"You can't see how lonely I am." When she offered nothing to this speech, he enlarged on it. "When it gets unbearable," he said, "I sit in front of the mirror and keep myself company. If that doesn't make your heart ache, nothing will."

"I'm afraid I have a heart-ache, but it is not that." For a terrible moment he thought of that theory of his which referred to a disappointment in love. Was she going to have the unbelievable cruelty to tell him about it?

"I have to talk to somebody," she said simply. "And I came to you, because you've worked on a newspaper, and you have had a lot of experience. It's—a matter of ethics. But really it's a matter of life and death."

He felt most horribly humble before her, and he hated the lie, except that it had brought her to him. There was something so direct and childlike about her. The very way she drew a chair in front of him, and proceeded, talking rather fast, to lay the matter before him, touched him profoundly. He felt, somehow, incredibly old and experienced.

And then, after all that, to fail her!

"You see how it is," she finished. "I can't go to the Staff, and they wouldn't do anything if I did—except possibly put me out. Because a nurse really only follows orders. And—I've got to stay, if I can. And Doctor Willie doesn't believe in an operation and won't see that he's dying. And everybody at home thinks he is right, because—well," she added hastily, "he's been right a good many times."

He listened attentively. His record, you remember, was his own way some ninety-seven per cent of the time, and at first he would not believe that this was going to be the three per cent, or a part of it.

"Well," he said at last, "we'll just make the Staff turn in and do it. That's easy."

"But they won't. They can't."

"We can't let Johnny die, either, can we?"

But when at last she was gone, and the room was incredibly empty without her,—when, to confess a fact that he was exceedingly shame-faced about, he had wheeled over to the chair she had sat in and put his cheek against the arm where her hand had rested, when he was somewhat his own man again and had got over the feeling that his arms were empty of something they had never held—then it was that Twenty-two found himself up against the three per cent.

The hospital's attitude was firm. It could not interfere. It was an outside patient and an outside doctor. Its responsibility ended with providing for the care of the patient, under his physician's orders. It was regretful—but, of course, unless the case was turned over to the Staff— —

He went back to the ward to tell her, after it had all been explained to him. But she was not surprised. He saw that, after all, she had really known he was going to fail her.

"It's hopeless," was all she said. "Everybody is right, and everybody is wrong."

It was the next day that, going to the courtyard for a breath of air, she saw a woman outside the iron gate waving to her. It was Johnny's mother, a forlorn old soul in what Jane Brown recognised as an old suit of her mother's.

"Doctor Willie bought my ticket, Miss Nellie," she said nervously. "It seems like I had to come, even if I couldn't get in. I've been waiting around most all afternoon. How is he?"

"He is resting quietly," said Jane Brown, holding herself very tense, because she wanted to scream. "He isn't suffering at all."

"Could you tell me which window he's near, Miss Nellie?"

She pointed out the window, and Johnny Fraser's mother stood, holding to the bars, peering up at it. Her lips moved, and Jane Brown knew that she was praying. At last she turned her eyes away.

"Folks have said a lot about him," she said, "but he was always a good son to me. If only he'd had a chance—I'd be right worried, Miss Nellie, if he didn't have Doctor Willie looking after him."

Jane Brown went into the building. There was just one thing clear in her mind. Johnny Fraser must have his chance, somehow.

In the meantime things were not doing any too well in the hospital. A second case, although mild, had extended the quarantine. Discontent grew, and threatened to develop into mutiny. Six men from one of the wards marched en masse to the lower hall, and were preparing to rush the guards when they were discovered. The Senior Surgical Interne took two prisoners himself, and became an emergency case for two stitches and arnica compresses.

Jane Brown helped to fix him up, and he took advantage of her holding a dressing basin near his cut lip to kiss her hand, very respectfully. She would have resented it under other circumstances, but the Senior Surgical

Interne was, even if temporarily, a patient, and must be humoured. She forgot about the kiss immediately, anyhow, although he did not.

Her three months of probation were drawing to a close now, and her cap was already made and put away in a box, ready for the day she should don it. But she did not look at it very often.

And all the time, fighting his battle with youth and vigour, but with closed eyes, and losing it day by day, was Johnny Fraser.

Then, one night on the roof, Jane Brown had to refuse the Senior Surgical Interne. He took it very hard.

"We'd have been such pals," he said, rather wistfully, after he saw it was no use.

"We can be, anyhow."

"I suppose," he said with some bitterness, "that I'd have stood a better chance if I'd done as you wanted me to about that fellow in your ward, gone to the staff and raised hell."

"I wouldn't have married you," said Jane Brown, "but I'd have thought you were pretty much of a man."

The more he thought about that the less he liked it. It almost kept him awake that night.

It was the next day that Twenty-two had his idea. He ran true to form, and carried it back to Jane Brown for her approval. But she was not enthusiastic.

"It would help to amuse them, of course, but how can you publish a newspaper without any news?" she asked, rather listlessly, for her.

"News! This building is full of news. I have some bits already. Listen!" He took a notebook out of his pocket. "The stork breaks quarantine. New baby in O ward. The chief engineer has developed a boil on his neck. Elevator

Man arrested for breaking speed limit. Wanted, four square inches of cuticle for skin grafting in W. How's that? And I'm only beginning."

Jane Brown listened. Somehow, behind Twenty-two's lightness of tone, she felt something more earnest. She did not put it into words, even to herself, but she divined something new, a desire to do his bit, there in the hospital. It was, if she had only known it, a milestone in a hitherto unmarked career. Twenty-two, who had always been a man, was by way of becoming a person.

He explained about publishing it. He used to run a typewriter in college, and the convalescents could mimeograph it and sell it. There was a mimeographing machine in the office.

The Senior Surgical Interne came in just then. Refusing to marry him had had much the effect of smacking a puppy. He came back, a trifle timid, but friendly. So he came in just then, and elected himself to the advertising and circulation department, and gave the Probationer the society end, although it was not his paper or his idea, and sat down at once at the table and started a limerick, commencing:

"We're here in the city, marooned"

However, he never got any further with it, because there are, apparently, no rhymes for "marooned." He refused "tuned" which several people offered him, with extreme scorn.

Up to this point Jane Brown had been rather too worried to think about Twenty-two. She had grown accustomed to seeing him coming slowly back toward her ward, his eyes travelling much faster than he did. Not, of course, that she knew that. And to his being, in a way, underfoot a part of every day, after the Head had made rounds and was safely out of the road for a good two hours.

But two things happened that day to turn her mind in onto her heart. One was when she heard about the artificial leg. The other was when she passed the door of his room, where a large card now announced "Office of the Quarantine Sentinel." She passed the door, and she distinctly heard most un-hospital-like chatter within. Judging from the shadows on the glass door, too, the room was full. It sounded joyous and carefree.

Something in Jane Brown—her mind, probably—turned right around and looked into her heart, and made an odd discovery. This was that Jane Brown's heart had sunk about two inches, and was feeling very queer.

She went straight on, however, and put on a fresh collar in her little bedroom, and listed her washing and changed her shoes, because her feet still ached a lot of the time. But she was a brave person and liked to look things in the face. So before she went back to the ward, she stood in front of her mirror and said:

"You're a nice nurse, Nell Brown. To—to talk about duty and brag about service, and then to act like a fool."

She went back to the ward and sat beside Johnny. But that night she went up on the roof again, and sat on the parapet. She could see, across the courtyard, the dim rectangles of her ward, and around a corner in plain view, "room Twenty-two." Its occupant was sitting at the typewriter, and working hard. Or he seemed to be. It was too far away to be sure. Jane Brown slid down onto the roof, which was not very clean, and putting her elbows on the parapet, watched him for a long time. When he got up, at last, and came to the open window, she hardly breathed. However, he only stood there, looking toward her but not seeing her.

Jane Brown put her head on the parapet that night and cried. She thought she was crying about Johnny Fraser. She might have felt somewhat comforted had she known that Twenty-two, being tired with his day's work, had at last given way to most horrible jealousy of the Senior Surgical Interne, and that his misery was to hers as five is to one.

The first number of the Quarantine Sentinel was a great success. It served in the wards much the same purpose as the magazines published in the trenches. It relieved the monotony, brought the different wards together, furnished laughter and gossip. Twenty-two wrote the editorials, published the paper, with the aid of a couple of convalescents, and in his leisure drew cartoons. He drew very well, but all his girls looked like Jane Brown. It caused a ripple of talk.

The children from the children's ward distributed them, and went back from the private rooms bearing tribute of flowers and fruit. Twenty-two himself developed a most reprehensible habit of concealing candy in the Sentinel office and smuggling it to his carriers. Altogether a new and neighbourly feeling seemed to follow in the wake of the little paper. People who had sulked in side-by-side rooms began, in the relaxed discipline of convalescence, to pay little calls about. Crotchety dowagers knitted socks for new babies. A wave of friendliness swept over every one, and engulfed particularly Twenty-two.

In the glow of it he changed perceptibly. This was the first popularity he had ever earned, and the first he had ever cared a fi-penny bit about. And, because he valued it, he felt more and more unworthy of it.

But it kept him from seeing Jane Brown. He was too busy for many excursions to the ward, and when he went he was immediately the centre of an animated group. He hardly ever saw her alone, and when he did he began to suspect that she pretended duties that might have waited.

One day he happened to go back while Doctor Willie was there, and after that he understood her problem better.

Through it all Johnny lived. His thin, young body was now hardly an outline under the smooth, white covering of his bed. He swallowed, faintly, such bits of liquid as were placed between his lips, but there were times when Jane Brown's fingers, more expert now, could find no pulse at all. And still she had found no way to give him his chance.

She made a last appeal to Doctor Willie that day, but he only shook his head gravely.

"Even if there was an operation now, Nellie," said Doctor Willie that day, "he could not stand it."

It was the first time that Twenty-two had known her name was Nellie.

That was the last day of Jane Brown's probation. On the next day she was to don her cap. The Sentinel came out with a congratulatory editorial, and at nine o'clock that night the First Assistant brought an announcement, in the Head's own writing, for the paper.

"The Head of the Training School announces with much pleasure the acceptance of Miss N. Jane Brown as a pupil nurse."

Twenty-two sat and stared at it for quite a long time.

That night Jane Brown fought her battle and won. She went to her room immediately after chapel, and took the family pictures off her little stand and got out ink and paper. She put the photographs out of sight, because she knew that they were counting on her, and she could not bear her mother's eyes. And then she counted her money, because she had broken another thermometer, and the ticket home was rather expensive. She had enough, but very little more.

After that she went to work.

It took her rather a long time, because she had a great deal to explain. She had to put her case, in fact. And she was not strong on either ethics or logic. She said so, indeed, at the beginning. She said also that she had talked to a lot of people, but that no one understood how she felt — that there ought to be no professional ethics, or etiquette, or anything else, where it was life or death. That she felt hospitals were to save lives and not to save feelings. It seemed necessary, after that, to defend Doctor Willie — without naming him, of course. How much good he had done, and how he came to rely on himself and his own opinion because in the country there was no one to consult with.

However, she was not so gentle with the Staff. She said that it was standing by and letting a patient die, because it was too polite to interfere, although they had all agreed among themselves that an operation was necessary. And that if they felt that way, would they refuse to pull a child from in front of a locomotive because it was its mother's business, and she didn't know how to do it?

Then she signed it.

She turned it in at the Sentinel office the next morning while the editor was shaving. She had to pass it through a crack in the door. Even that, however, was enough for the editor in question to see that she wore no cap.

"But—see here," he said, in a rather lathery voice, "you're accepted, you know. Where's the—the visible sign?"

Jane Brown was not quite sure she could speak. However, she managed.

"After you read that," she said, "you'll understand."

He read it immediately, of course, growing more and more grave, and the soap drying on his chin. Its sheer courage made him gasp.

"Good girl," he said to himself. "Brave little girl. But it finishes her here, and she knows it."

He was pretty well cut up about it, too, because while he was getting it ready he felt as if he was sharpening a knife to stab her with. Her own knife, too. But he had to be as brave as she was.

The paper came out at two o'clock. At three the First Assistant, looking extremely white, relieved Jane Brown of the care of H ward and sent her to her room.

Jane Brown eyed her wistfully.

"I'm not to come back, I suppose?"

The First Assistant avoided her eyes.

"I'm afraid not," she said.

Jane Brown went up the ward and looked down at Johnny Fraser. Then she gathered up her bandage scissors and her little dressing forceps and went out.

The First Assistant took a step after her, but stopped. There were tears in her eyes.

Things moved very rapidly in the hospital that day, while the guards sat outside on their camp-stools and ate apples or read the newspapers, and while Jane Brown sat alone in her room.

First of all the Staff met and summoned Twenty-two. He went down in the elevator — he had lost Elizabeth a few days before, and was using a cane — ready for trouble. He had always met a fight more than halfway. It was the same instinct that had taken him to the fire.

But no one wanted to fight. The Staff was waiting, grave and perplexed, but rather anxious to put its case than otherwise. It felt misunderstood, aggrieved, and horribly afraid it was going to get in the newspapers. But it was not angry. On the contrary, it was trying its extremely intelligent best to see things from a new angle.

The Senior Surgical Interne was waiting outside. He had smoked eighteen cigarettes since he received his copy of the Sentinel, and was as unhappy as an interne can be.

"What the devil made you publish it?" he demanded.

Twenty-two smiled.

"Because," he said, "I have always had a sneaking desire to publish an honest paper, one where public questions can be discussed. If this isn't a public question, I don't know one when I see it."

But he was not smiling when he went in.

An hour later Doctor Willie came in. He had brought some flowers for the children's ward, and his arms were bulging. To his surprise, accustomed as he was to the somewhat cavalier treatment of the country practitioner in a big city hospital, he was invited to the Staff room.

To the eternal credit of the Staff Jane Brown's part in that painful half hour was never known. The Staff was careful, too, of Doctor Willie. They knew they were being irregular, and were most wretchedly uncomfortable. Also, there being six of them against one, it looked rather like force, particularly since, after the first two minutes, every one of them liked Doctor Willie.

He took it so awfully well. He sat there, with his elbows on a table beside a withering mass of spring flowers, and faced the white-coated Staff, and said that he hoped he was man enough to acknowledge a mistake, and six opinions against one left him nothing else to do. The Senior Surgical Interne, who had been hating him for weeks, offered him a cigar.

He had only one request to make. There was a little girl in the training school who believed in him, and he would like to go to the ward and write the order for the operation himself.

Which he did. But Jane Brown was not there.

Late that evening the First Assistant, passing along the corridor in the dormitory, was accosted by a quiet figure in a blue uniform, without a cap.

"How is he?"

The First Assistant was feeling more cheerful than usual. The operating surgeon had congratulated her on the way things had moved that day, and she was feeling, as she often did, that, after all, work was a solace for many troubles.

"Of course, it is very soon, but he stood it well." She looked up at Jane Brown, who was taller than she was, but who always, somehow, looked rather little. There are girls like that. "Look here," she said, "you must not sit in that room and worry. Run up to the operating-room and help to clear away."

She was very wise, the First Assistant. For Jane Brown went, and washed away some of the ache with the stains of Johnny's operation. Here, all about her, were the tangible evidences of her triumph, which was also a defeat. A little glow of service revived in her. If Johnny lived, it was a small price to pay for a life. If he died, she had given him his chance. The operating-room nurses were very kind. They liked her courage, but they were frightened, too. She, like the others, had been right, but also she was wrong.

They paid her tribute of little kindnesses, but they knew she must go.

It was the night nurse who told Twenty-two that Jane Brown was in the operating-room. He was still up and dressed at midnight, but the sheets of to-morrow's editorial lay blank on his table.

The night nurse glanced at her watch to see if it was time for the twelve o'clock medicines.

"There's a rumour going about," she said, "that the quarantine's to be lifted to-morrow. I'll be rather sorry. It has been a change."

"To-morrow," said Twenty-two, in a startled voice.

"I suppose you'll be going out at once?"

There was a wistful note in her voice. She liked him. He had been an oasis of cheer in the dreary rounds of the night. A very little more, and she might have forgotten her rule, which was never to be sentimentally interested in a patient.

"I wonder," said Twenty-two, in a curious tone, "if you will give me my cane?"

He was clad, at that time, in a hideous bathrobe, purchased by the orderly, over his night clothing, and he had the expression of a person who intends to take no chances.

"Thanks," said Twenty-two. "And—will you send the night watchman here?"

The night nurse went out. She had a distinct feeling that something was about to happen. At least she claimed it later. But she found the night watchman making coffee in a back pantry, and gave him her message.

Some time later Jane Brown stood in the doorway of the operating-room and gave it a farewell look. Its white floor and walls were spotless. Shining rows of instruments on clean towels were ready to put away in the cabinets. The sterilisers glowed in warm rectangles of gleaming copper. Over all brooded the peace of order, the quiet of the night.

Outside the operating-room door she drew a long breath, and faced the night watchman. She had left something in Twenty-two. Would she go and get it?

"It's very late," said Jane Brown. "And it isn't allowed, I'm sure."

However, what was one more rule to her who had defied them all? A spirit of recklessness seized her. After all, why not? She would never see him again. Like the operating-room, she would stand in the doorway and say a mute little farewell.

Twenty-two's door was wide open, and he was standing in the centre of the room, looking out. He had heard her long before she came in sight, for he, too, had learned the hospital habit of classifying footsteps.

He was horribly excited. He had never been so nervous before. He had made up a small speech, a sort of beginning, but he forgot it the moment he heard her, and she surprised him in the midst of trying, agonisingly, to remember it.

There was a sort of dreadful calm, however, about Jane Brown.

"The watchman says I have left something here."

It was clear to him at once that he meant nothing to her. It was in her voice.

"You did," he said. And tried to smile.

"Then—if I may have it——"

"I wish to heaven you could have it," he said, very rapidly. "I don't want it. It's darned miserable."

"It's—what?"

"It's an ache," he went on, still rather incoherent. "A pain. A misery." Then, seeing her beginning to put on a professional look: "No, not that. It's a feeling. Look here," he said, rather more slowly, "do you mind coming in and closing the door? There's a man across who's always listening."

She went in, but she did not close the door. She went slowly, looking rather pale.

"What I sent for you for is this," said Twenty-two, "are you going away? Because I've got to know."

"I'm being sent away as soon as the quarantine is over. It's—it's perfectly right. I expected it. Things would soon go to pieces if the nurses took to—took to doing what I did."

Suddenly Twenty-two limped across the room and slammed the door shut, a proceeding immediately followed by an irritated ringing of bells at the night nurse's desk. Then he turned, his back against the door.

"Because I'm going when you do," he said, in a terrible voice. "I'm going when you go, and wherever you go. I've stood all the waiting around for a glimpse of you that I'm going to stand." He glared at her. "For weeks," he said, "I've sat here in this room and listened for you, and hated to go to sleep for fear you would pass and I wouldn't be looking through that damned door. And now I've reached the limit."

A sort of band which had seemed to be fastened around Jane Brown's head for days suddenly removed itself to her heart, which became extremely irregular.

"And I want to say this," went on Twenty-two, still in a savage tone. He was horribly frightened, so he blustered. "I don't care whether you want me or not, you've got to have me. I'm so much in love with you that it hurts."

Suddenly Jane Brown's heart settled down into a soft rhythmic beating that was like a song. After all, life was made up of love and work, and love came first.

She faced Twenty-two with brave eyes.

"I love you, too—so much that it hurts."

The gentleman across the hall, sitting up in bed, with an angry thumb on the bell, was electrified to see, on the glass door across, the silhouette of a young lady without a cap go into the arms of a very large, masculine silhouette in a dressing-gown. He heard, too, the thump of a falling cane.

Late that night Jane Brown, by devious ways, made her way back to H ward. Johnny was there, a strange Johnny with a bandaged head, but with open eyes.

At dawn, the dawn of the day when Jane Brown was to leave the little world of the hospital for a little world of two, consisting of a man and a woman, the night nurse found her there, asleep, her fingers still on Johnny's thin wrist.

She did not report it.

JANE

I

Having retired to a hospital to sulk, Jane remained there. The family came and sat by her bed uncomfortably and smoked, and finally retreated with defeat written large all over it, leaving Jane to the continued possession of Room 33, a pink kimono with slippers to match, a hand-embroidered face pillow with a rose-coloured bow on the corner, and a young nurse with a gift of giving Jane daily the appearance of a strawberry and vanilla ice rising from a meringue of bed linen.

Jane's complaint was temper. The family knew this, and so did Jane, although she had an annoying way of looking hurt, a gentle heart-brokenness of speech that made the family, under the pretence of getting a match, go out into the hall and swear softly under its breath. But it was temper, and the family was not deceived. Also, knowing Jane, the family was quite ready to believe that while it was swearing in the hall, Jane was biting holes in the hand-embroidered face pillow in Room 33.

It had finally come to be a test of endurance. Jane vowed to stay at the hospital until the family on bended knee begged her to emerge and to brighten the world again with her presence. The family, being her father, said it would be damned if it would, and that if Jane cared to live on anæmic chicken broth, oatmeal wafers and massage twice a day for the rest of her life, why, let her.

The dispute, having begun about whether Jane should or should not marry a certain person, Jane representing the affirmative and her father the negative, had taken on new aspects, had grown and altered, and had, to be brief, become a contest between the masculine Johnson and the feminine Johnson as to which would take the count. Not that this appeared on the surface. The masculine Johnson, having closed the summer home on Jane's defection and gone back to the city, sent daily telegrams, novels and hothouse grapes, all three of which Jane devoured indiscriminately. Once, indeed, Father Johnson had motored the forty miles from town, to be told that Jane was too ill and unhappy to see him, and to have a glimpse, as he drove furiously away, of Jane sitting pensive at her window in the pink kimono, gazing over his head at the distant hills and clearly entirely indifferent to him and his wrath.

So we find Jane, on a frosty morning in late October, in triumphant possession of the field—aunts and cousins routed, her father sulking in town, and the victor herself—or is victor feminine?—and if it isn't, shouldn't it be?—sitting up in bed staring blankly at her watch.

Jane had just wakened—an hour later than usual; she had rung the bell three times and no one had responded. Jane's famous temper began to stretch and yawn. At this hour Jane was accustomed to be washed with tepid water, scented daintily with violet, alcohol-rubbed, talcum-powdered, and finally fresh-linened, coifed and manicured, to be supported with a heap of fresh pillows and fed creamed sweet-bread and golden-brown coffee and toast.

Jane rang again, with a line between her eyebrows. The bell was not broken. She could hear it distinctly. This was an outrage! She would report it to the superintendent. She had been ringing for ten minutes. That little minx of a nurse was flirting somewhere with one of the internes.

Jane angrily flung the covers back and got out on her small bare feet. Then she stretched her slim young arms above her head, her spoiled red mouth forming a scarlet O as she yawned. In her sleeveless and neckless nightgown, with her hair over her shoulders, minus the more elaborate coiffure which later in the day helped her to poise and firmness, she looked a pretty young girl, almost—although Jane herself never suspected this—almost an amiable young person.

Jane saw herself in the glass and assumed immediately the two lines between her eyebrows which were the outward and visible token of what she had suffered. Then she found her slippers, a pair of stockings to match and two round bits of pink silk elastic of private and feminine use, and sat down on the floor to put them on.

The floor was cold. To Jane's wrath was added indignation. She hitched herself along the boards to the radiator and put her hand on it. It was even colder than Jane.

The family temper was fully awake by this time and ready for business. Jane, sitting on the icy floor, jerked on her stockings, snapped the pink bands into place, thrust her feet into her slippers and rose, shivering. She went to the bed, and by dint of careful manœuvring so placed the bell between the head of the bed and the wall that during the remainder of her toilet it rang steadily.

The remainder of Jane's toilet was rather casual. She flung on the silk kimono, twisted her hair on top of her head and stuck a pin or two in it, thus achieving a sort of effect a thousand times more bewildering than she had ever managed with a curling iron and twenty seven hair pins, and flinging her door wide stalked into the hall. At least she meant to stalk, but one does not really stamp about much in number-two, heelless, pink-satin mules.

At the first stalk—or stamp—she stopped. Standing uncertainly just outside her door was a strange man, strangely attired. Jane clutched her kimono about her and stared.

"Did—did you—are you ringing?" asked the apparition. It wore a pair of white-duck trousers, much soiled, a coat that bore the words "furnace room" down the front in red letters on a white tape, and a clean and spotless white apron. There was coal dust on its face and streaks of it in its hair, which appeared normally to be red.

"There's something the matter with your bell," said the young man. "It keeps on ringing."

"I intend it to," said Jane coldly.

"You can't make a racket like that round here, you know," he asserted, looking past her into the room.

"I intend to make all the racket I can until I get some attention."

"What have you done—put a book on it?"

"Look here"—Jane added another line to the two between her eyebrows. In the family this was generally a signal for a retreat, but of course the young man could not know this, and, besides, he was red-headed. "Look here," said Jane, "I don't know who you are and I don't care either, but that bell is going to ring until I get my bath and some breakfast. And it's going to ring then unless I stop it."

The young man in the coal dust and the white apron looked at Jane and smiled. Then he walked past her into the room, jerked the bed from the wall and released the bell.

"Now!" he said as the din outside ceased. "I'm too busy to talk just at present, but if you do that again I'll take the bell out of the room altogether. There are other people in the hospital besides yourself."

At that he started out and along the hall, leaving Jane speechless. After he'd gone about a dozen feet he stopped and turned, looking at Jane reflectively.

"Do you know anything about cooking?" he asked.

"I know more about cooking than you do about politeness," she retorted, white with fury, and went into her room and slammed the door. She went directly to the bell and put it behind the bed and set it to ringing again. Then she sat down in a chair and picked up a book. Had the red-haired person opened the door she was perfectly prepared to fling the book at him. She would have thrown a hatchet had she had one.

As a matter of fact, however, he did not come back. The bell rang with a soul-satisfying jangle for about two minutes and then died away, and no amount of poking with a hairpin did any good. It was clear that the bell had been cut off outside!

For fifty-five minutes Jane sat in that chair breakfastless, very casually washed and with the aforesaid Billie Burkeness of hair. Then, hunger gaining over temper, she opened the door and peered out. From somewhere near at hand there came a pungent odor of burning toast. Jane sniffed; then, driven by hunger, she made a short sally down the hall to the parlour where the nurses on duty made their headquarters. It was empty. The dismantled bell register was on the wall, with the bell unscrewed and lying on the mantel beside it, and the odour of burning toast was stronger than ever.

Jane padded softly to the odour, following her small nose. It led her to the pantry, where under ordinary circumstances the patients' trays were prepared by a pantrymaid, the food being shipped there from the kitchen on a lift. Clearly the circumstances were not ordinary. The pantrymaid was not in sight.

Instead, the red-haired person was standing by the window scraping busily at a blackened piece of toast. There was a rank odour of boiling tea in the air.

"Damnation!" said the red-haired person, and flung the toast into a corner where there already lay a small heap of charred breakfast hopes. Then he saw Jane.

"I fixed the bell, didn't I?" he remarked. "I say, since you claim to know so much about cooking, I wish you'd make some toast."

"I didn't say I knew much," snapped Jane, holding her kimono round her. "I said I knew more than you knew about politeness."

The red-haired person smiled again, and then, making a deep bow, with a knife in one hand and a toaster in the other, he said: "Madam, I prithee forgive me for my untoward conduct of an hour since. Say but the word and I replace the bell."

"I won't make any toast," said Jane, looking at the bread with famished eyes.

"Oh, very well," said the red-haired person with a sigh. "On your head be it!"

"But I'll tell you how to do it," conceded Jane, "if you'll explain who you are and what you are doing in that costume and where the nurses are."

The red-haired person sat down on the edge of the table and looked at her.

"I'll make a bargain with you," he said. "There's a convalescent typhoid in a room near yours who swears he'll go down to the village for something to eat in his—er—hospital attire unless he's fed soon. He's dangerous, empty. He's reached the cannibalistic stage. If he should see you in that ravishing pink thing, I—I wouldn't answer for the consequences. I'll tell you everything if you'll make him six large slices of toast and boil him four or five eggs, enough to hold him for a while. The tea's probably ready; it's been boiling for an hour."

Hunger was making Jane human. She gathered up the tail of her kimono, and stepping daintily into the pantry proceeded to spread herself a slice of bread and butter.

"Where is everybody?" she asked, licking some butter off her thumb with a small pink tongue.

Oh, I am the cook and the captain bold,

    And the mate of the Nancy brig,

And the bosun tight and the midshipmite,

    And the crew of the captain's gig.

recited the red-haired person.

"You!" said Jane with the bread halfway to her mouth.

"Even I," said the red-haired person. "I'm the superintendent, the staff, the training school, the cooks, the furnace man and the ambulance driver."

Jane was pouring herself a cup of tea, and she put in milk and sugar and took a sip or two before she would give him the satisfaction of asking him what he meant. Anyhow, probably she had already guessed. Jane was no fool.

"I hope you're getting the salary list," she said, sitting on the pantry girl's chair and, what with the tea inside and somebody to quarrel with, feeling more like herself. "My father's one of the directors, and somebody gets it."

The red-haired person sat on the radiator and eyed Jane. He looked slightly stunned, as if the presence of beauty in a Billie Burke chignon and little else except a kimono was almost too much for him. From somewhere near by came a terrific thumping, as of some one pounding a hairbrush on a table. The red-haired person shifted along the radiator a little nearer Jane, and continued to gloat.

"Don't let that noise bother you," he said; "that's only the convalescent typhoid banging for his breakfast. He's been shouting for food ever since I came at six last night."

"Is it safe to feed him so much?"

"I don't know. He hasn't had anything yet. Perhaps if you're ready you'd better fix him something."

Jane had finished her bread and tea by this time and remembered her kimono.

"I'll go back and dress," she said primly. But he wouldn't hear of it.

"He's starving," he objected as a fresh volley of thumps came along the hall. "I've been trying at intervals since daylight to make him a piece of toast. The minute I put it on the fire I think of something I've forgotten, and when I come back it's in flames."

So Jane cut some bread and put on eggs to boil, and the red-haired person told his story.

"You see," he explained, "although I appear to be a furnace man from the waist up and an interne from the waist down, I am really the new superintendent."

"I hope you'll do better than the last one," she said severely. "He was always flirting with the nurses."

"I shall never flirt with the nurses," he promised, looking at her. "Anyhow I shan't have any immediate chance. The other fellow left last night and took with him everything portable except the ambulance—nurses, staff, cooks. I wish to Heaven he'd taken the patients! And he did more than that. He cut the telephone wires!"

"Well!" said Jane. "Are you going to stand for it?"

The red-haired man threw up his hands. "The village is with him," he declared. "It's a factional fight—the village against the fashionable summer colony on the hill. I cannot telephone from the village—the telegraph operator is deaf when I speak to him; the village milkman and grocer sent boys up this morning—look here." He fished a scrap of paper from his pocket and read:

I will not supply the Valley Hospital with any fresh meats, canned oysters and sausages, or do any plumbing for the hospital until the reinstatement of Dr. Sheets.

T. CASHDOLLAR, Butcher.

Jane took the paper and read it again. "Humph!" she commented. "Old Sheets wrote it himself. Mr. Cashdollar couldn't think 'reinstatement,' let alone spell it."

"The question is not who wrote it, but what we are to do," said the red-haired person. "Shall I let old Sheets come back?"

"If you do," said Jane fiercely, "I shall hate you the rest of my life."

And as it was clear by this time that the red-haired person could imagine nothing more horrible, it was settled then and there that he should stay.

"There are only two wards," he said. "In the men's a man named Higgins is able to be up and is keeping things straight. And in the woman's ward Mary O'Shaughnessy is looking after them. The furnaces are the worst. I'd have forgiven almost anything else. I've sat up all night nursing the fires, but they breathed their last at six this morning and I guess there's nothing left but to call the coroner."

Jane had achieved a tolerable plate of toast by that time and four eggs. Also she had a fine flush, a combination of heat from the gas stove and temper.

"They ought to be ashamed," she cried angrily, "leaving a lot of sick people!"

"Oh, as to that," said the red-headed person, "there aren't any very sick ones. Two or three neurasthenics like yourself and a convalescent typhoid and a D.T. in a private room. If it wasn't that Mary O'Shaughnessy — —"

But at the word "neurasthenics" Jane had put down the toaster, and by the time the unconscious young man had reached the O'Shaughnessy she was going out the door with her chin up. He called after her, and finding she did not turn he followed her, shouting apologies at her back until she went into her room. And as hospital doors don't lock from the inside she pushed the washstand against the knob and went to bed to keep warm.

He stood outside and apologised again, and later he brought a tray of bread and butter and a pot of the tea, which had been boiling for two hours by that time, and put it outside the door on the floor. But Jane refused to get it, and finished her breakfast from a jar of candied ginger that some one had sent her, and read "Lorna Doone."

Now and then a sound of terrific hammering would follow the steampipes and Jane would smile wickedly. By noon she had finished the ginger and was wondering what the person about whom she and the family had disagreed would think when he heard the way she was being treated. And by one o'clock she had cried her eyes entirely shut and had pushed the washstand back from the door.

II

Now a hospital full of nurses and doctors with a bell to summon food and attention is one thing. A hospital without nurses and doctors, and with only one person to do everything, and that person mostly in the cellar, is quite another. Jane was very sad and lonely, and to add to her troubles the delirium-tremens case down the hall began to sing "Oh Promise Me" in a falsetto voice and kept it up for hours.

At three Jane got up and bathed her eyes. She also did her hair, and thus fortified she started out to find the red-haired person. She intended to say that she was paying sixty-five dollars a week and belonged to a leading family, and that she didn't mean to endure for a moment the treatment she was getting, and being called a neurasthenic and made to cook for the other patients.

She went slowly along the hall. The convalescent typhoid heard her and called.

"Hey, doc!" he cried. "Hey, doc! Great Scott, man, when do I get some dinner?"

Jane quickened her steps and made for the pantry. From somewhere beyond, the delirium-tremens case was singing happily:

I—love you o—own—ly,

I love—but—you.

Jane shivered a little. The person in whom she had been interested and who had caused her precipitate retirement, if not to a nunnery, to what answered the same purpose, had been very fond of that song. He used to sing it, leaning over the piano and looking into her eyes.

Jane's nose led her again to the pantry. There was a sort of soupy odour in the air, and sure enough the red-haired person was there, very immaculate in fresh ducks, pouring boiling water into three tea-cups out of a kettle and then dropping a beef capsule into each cup.

Now Jane had intended, as I have said, to say that she was being outrageously treated, and belonged to one of the best families, and so on. What she really said was piteously:

"How good it smells!"

"Doesn't it!" said the red-haired person, sniffing. "Beef capsules. I've made thirty cups of it so far since one o'clock—the more they have the more they want. I say, be a good girl and run up to the kitchen for some more crackers while I carry food to the convalescent typhoid. He's murderous!"

"Where are the crackers?" asked Jane stiffly, but not exactly caring to raise an issue until she was sure of getting something to eat.

"Store closet in the kitchen, third drawer on the left," said the red-haired man, shaking some cayenne pepper into one of the cups. "You might stop that howling lunatic on your way if you will."

"How?" asked Jane, pausing.

"Ram a towel down his throat, or—but don't bother. I'll dose him with this beef tea and red pepper, and he'll be too busy putting out the fire to want to sing."

"You wouldn't be so cruel!" said Jane, rather drawing back. The red-haired person smiled and to Jane it showed that he was actually ferocious. She ran all the way up for the crackers and down again, carrying the tin box. There is no doubt that Jane's family would have promptly swooned had it seen her.

When she came down there was a sort of after-dinner peace reigning. The convalescent typhoid, having filled up on milk and beef soup, had floated off to sleep. "The Chocolate Soldier" had given way to deep-muttered imprecations from the singer's room. Jane made herself a cup of bouillon and drank it scalding. She was making the second when the red-haired person came back with an empty cup.

"I forgot to explain," he said, "that beef tea and red pepper's the treatment for our young friend in there. After a man has been burning his stomach daily with a quart or so of raw booze — — "

"I beg your pardon," said Jane coolly. Booze was not considered good form on the hill — the word, of course. There was plenty of the substance.

"Raw booze," repeated the red-haired person. "Nothing short of red pepper or dynamite is going to act as a substitute. Why, I'll bet the inside of that chap's stomach is of the general sensitiveness and consistency of my shoe."

"Indeed!" said Jane, coldly polite. In Jane's circle people did not discuss the interiors of other people's stomachs. The red-haired person sat on the table with a cup of bouillon in one hand and a cracker in the other.

"You know," he said genially, "it's awfully bully of you to come out and keep me company like this. I never put in such a day. I've given up fussing with the furnace and got out extra blankets instead. And I think by night our troubles will be over." He held up the cup and glanced at Jane, who was looking entrancingly pretty. "To our troubles being over!" he said, draining the cup, and then found that he had used the red pepper again by mistake. It took five minutes and four cups of cold water to enable him to explain what he meant.

"By our troubles being over," he said finally when he could speak, "I mean this: There's a train from town at eight to-night, and if all goes well it will deposit in the village half a dozen nurses, a cook or two, a furnace man — good Heavens, I wonder if I forgot a furnace man!"

It seemed, as Jane discovered, that the telephone wires being cut, he had sent Higgins from the men's ward to the village to send some telegrams for him.

"I couldn't leave, you see," he explained, "and having some small reason to believe that I am persona non grata in this vicinity I sent Higgins."

Jane had always hated the name Higgins. She said afterward that she felt uneasy from that moment. The red-haired person, who was not bad-looking, being tall and straight and having a very decent nose, looked at Jane, and Jane, having been shut away for weeks—Jane preened a little and was glad she had done her hair.

"You looked better the other way," said the red-haired person, reading her mind in a most uncanny manner. "Why should a girl with as pretty hair as yours cover it up with a net, anyhow?"

"You are very disagreeable and—and impertinent," said Jane, sliding off the table.

"It isn't disagreeable to tell a girl she has pretty hair," the red-haired person protested—"or impertinent either."

Jane was gathering up the remnants of her temper, scattered by the events of the day.

"You said I was a neurasthenic," she accused him. "It—it isn't being a neurasthenic to be nervous and upset and hating the very sight of people, is it?"

"Bless my soul!" said the red-haired man. "Then what is it?" Jane flushed, but he went on tactlessly: "I give you my word, I think you are the most perfectly"—he gave every appearance of being about to say "beautiful," but he evidently changed his mind—"the most perfectly healthy person I have ever looked at," he finished.

It is difficult to say just what Jane would have done under other circumstances, but just as she was getting her temper really in hand and preparing to launch something, shuffling footsteps were heard in the hall and Higgins stood in the doorway.

He was in a sad state. One of his eyes was entirely closed, and the corresponding ear stood out large and bulbous from his head. Also he was coated with mud, and he was carefully nursing one hand with the other.

He said he had been met at the near end of the railroad bridge by the ex-furnace man and one of the ex-orderlies and sent back firmly, having in fact been kicked back part of the way. He'd been told to report at the hospital that the tradespeople had instituted a boycott, and that either the former superintendent went back or the entire place could starve to death.

It was then that Jane discovered that her much-vaunted temper was not one-two-three to that of the red-haired person. He turned a sort of blue-white, shoved Jane out of his way as if she had been a chair, and she heard him clatter down the stairs and slam out of the front door.

Jane went back to her room and looked down the drive. He was running toward the bridge, and the sunlight on his red hair and his flying legs made him look like a revengeful meteor. Jane was weak in the knees. She knelt on the cold radiator and watched him out of sight, and then got trembly all over and fell to snivelling. This was of course because, if anything happened to him, she would be left entirely alone. And anyhow the D.T. case was singing again and had rather got on her nerves.

In ten minutes the red-haired person appeared. He had a wretched-looking creature by the back of the neck and he alternately pushed and kicked him up the drive. He—the red-haired person—was whistling and clearly immensely pleased with himself.

Jane put a little powder on her nose and waited for him to come and tell her all about it. But he did not come near. This was quite the cleverest thing he could have done, had he known it. Jane was not accustomed to waiting in vain. He must have gone directly to the cellar, half pushing and half kicking the luckless furnace man, for about four o'clock the radiator began to get warm.

At five he came and knocked at Jane's door, and on being invited in he sat down on the bed and looked at her.

"Well, we've got the furnace going," he said.

"Then that was the— —"

"Furnace man? Yes."

"Aren't you afraid to leave him?" queried Jane. "Won't he run off?"

"Got him locked in a padded cell," he said. "I can take him out to coal up. The rest of the time he can sit and think of his sins. The question is—what are we to do next?"

"I should think," ventured Jane, "that we'd better be thinking about supper."

"The beef capsules are gone."

"But surely there must be something else about—potatoes or things like that?"

He brightened perceptibly. "Oh, yes, carloads of potatoes, and there's canned stuff. Higgins can pare potatoes, and there's Mary O'Shaughnessy. We could have potatoes and canned tomatoes and eggs."

"Fine!" said Jane with her eyes gleaming, although the day before she would have said they were her three abominations.

And with that he called Higgins and Mary O'Shaughnessy and the four of them went to the kitchen.

Jane positively shone. She had never realised before how much she knew about cooking. They built a fire and got kettles boiling and everybody pared potatoes, and although in excess of zeal the eggs were ready long before everything else and the tomatoes scorched slightly, still they made up in enthusiasm what they lacked in ability, and when Higgins had carried the trays to the lift and started them on their way, Jane and the red-haired person shook hands on it and then ate a boiled potato from the same plate, sitting side by side on a table.

They were ravenous. They boiled one egg each and ate it, and then boiled another and another, and when they finished they found that Jane had eaten four potatoes, four eggs and unlimited bread and butter, while the red-haired person had eaten six saucers of stewed tomatoes and was starting on the seventh.

"You know," he said over the seventh, "we've got to figure this thing out. The entire town is solid against us—no use trying to get to a telephone. And anyhow they've got us surrounded. We're in a state of siege."

Jane was beating up an egg in milk for the D.T. patient, the capsules being exhausted, and the red-haired person was watching her closely. She had the two vertical lines between her eyes, but they looked really like lines of endeavour and not temper.

She stopped beating and looked up.

"Couldn't I go to the village?" she asked.

"They would stop you."

"Then—I think I know what we can do," she said, giving the eggnog a final whisk. "My people have a summer place on the hill. If you could get there you could telephone to the city."

"Could I get in?"

"I have a key."

Jane did not explain that the said key had been left by her father, with the terse hope that if she came to her senses she could get into the house and get her clothes.

"Good girl," said the red-headed person and patted her on the shoulder. "We'll euchre the old skate yet." Curiously, Jane did not resent either the speech or the pat.

He took the glass and tied on a white apron. "If our friend doesn't drink this, I will," he continued. "If he'd seen it in the making, as I have, he'd be crazy about it."

He opened the door and stood listening. From below floated up the refrain:

I—love you o—own—ly,

I love—but—you.

"Listen to that!" he said. "Stomach's gone, but still has a heart!"

Higgins came up the stairs heavily and stopped close by the red-haired person, whispering something to him. There was a second's pause. Then the red-haired person gave the eggnog to Higgins and both disappeared.

Jane was puzzled. She rather thought the furnace man had got out and listened for a scuffle, but none came. She did, however, hear the singing cease below, and then commence with renewed vigour, and she heard Higgins slowly remounting the stairs. He came in, with the empty glass and a sheepish expression. Part of the eggnog was distributed over his person.

"He wants his nurse, ma'am," said Higgins. "Wouldn't let me near him. Flung a pillow at me."

"Where is the doctor?" demanded Jane.

"Busy," replied Higgins. "One of the women is sick."

Jane was provoked. She had put some labour into the eggnog. But it shows the curious evolution going on in her that she got out the eggs and milk and made another one without protest. Then with her head up she carried it to the door.

"You might clear things away, Higgins," she said, and went down the stairs. Her heart was going rather fast. Most of the men Jane knew drank more or less, but this was different. She would have turned back halfway there had it not been for Higgins and for owning herself conquered. That was Jane's real weakness—she never owned herself beaten.

The singing had subsided to a low muttering. Jane stopped outside the door and took a fresh grip on her courage. Then she pushed the door open and went in.

The light was shaded, and at first the tossing figure on the bed was only a misty outline of greys and whites. She walked over, expecting a pillow at any moment and shielding the glass from attack with her hand.

"I have brought you another eggnog," she began severely, "and if you spill it——"

Then she looked down and saw the face on the pillow.

To her everlasting credit, Jane did not faint. But in that moment, while she stood staring down at the flushed young face with its tumbled dark hair and deep-cut lines of dissipation, the man who had sung to her over the piano, looking love into her eyes, died to her, and Jane, cold and steady, sat down on the side of the bed and fed the eggnog, spoonful by spoonful, to his corpse!

When the blank-eyed young man on the bed had swallowed it all passively, looking at her with dull, incurious eyes, she went back to her room and closing the door put the washstand against it. She did nothing theatrical. She went over to the window and stood looking out where the trees along the drive were fading in the dusk from green to grey, from grey to black. And over the transom came again and again monotonously the refrain:

I—love you o—own—ly,

I love—but—you.

Jane fell on her knees beside the bed and buried her wilful head in the hand-embroidered pillow, and said a little prayer because she had found out in time.

III

The full realisation of their predicament came with the dusk. The electric lights were shut off! Jane, crawling into bed tearfully at half after eight, turned the reading light switch over her head, but no flood of rosy radiance poured down on the hand-embroidered pillow with the pink bow.

Jane sat up and stared round her. Already the outline of her dresser was faint and shadowy. In half an hour black night would settle down and she had not even a candle or a box of matches. She crawled out, panicky, and began in the darkness to don her kimono and slippers. As she opened the door and stepped into the hall the convalescent typhoid heard her and set up his usual cry.

"Hey," he called, "whoever that is come in and fix the lights. They're broken. And I want some bread and milk. I can't sleep on an empty stomach!"

Jane padded on past the room where love lay cold and dead, down the corridor with its alarming echoes. The house seemed very quiet. At a corner unexpectedly she collided with some one going hastily. The result was a crash and a deluge of hot water. Jane got a drop on her bare ankle, and as soon as she could breathe she screamed.

"Why don't you look where you're going?" demanded the red-haired person angrily. "I've been an hour boiling that water, and now it has to be done over again!"

"It would do a lot of good to look!" retorted Jane. "But if you wish I'll carry a bell!"

"The thing for you to do," said the red-haired person severely, "is to go back to bed like a good girl and stay there until morning. The light is cut off."

"Really!" said Jane. "I thought it had just gone out for a walk. I daresay I may have a box of matches at least?"

He fumbled in his pockets without success.

"Not a match, of course!" he said disgustedly. "Was any one ever in such an infernal mess? Can't you get back to your room without matches?"

"I shan't go back at all unless I have some sort of light," maintained Jane. "I'm—horribly frightened!"

The break in her voice caught his attention and he put his hand out gently and took her arm.

"Now listen," he said. "You've been brave and fine all day, and don't stop it now. I—I've got all I can manage. Mary O'Shaughnessy is——" He stopped. "I'm going to be very busy," he said with half a groan. "I surely do wish you were forty for the next few hours. But you'll go back and stay in your room, won't you?"

He patted her arm, which Jane particularly hated generally. But Jane had altered considerably since morning.

"Then you cannot go to the telephone?"

"Not to-night."

"And Higgins?"

"Higgins has gone," he said. "He slipped off an hour ago. We'll have to manage to-night somehow. Now will you be a good child?"

"I'll go back," she promised meekly. "I'm sorry I'm not forty."

He turned her round and started her in the right direction with a little push. But she had gone only a step or two when she heard him coming after her quickly.

"Where are you?"

"Here," quavered Jane, not quite sure of him or of herself perhaps.

But when he stopped beside her he didn't try to touch her arm again. He only said:

"I wouldn't have you forty for anything in the world. I want you to be just as you are, very beautiful and young."

Then, as if he was afraid he would say too much, he turned on his heel, and a moment after he kicked against the fallen pitcher in the darkness and awoke a thousand echoes. As for Jane, she put her fingers to her ears and ran to her room, where she slammed the door and crawled into bed with burning cheeks.

Jane was never sure whether it was five minutes later or five seconds when somebody in the room spoke—from a chair by the window.

"Do you think," said a mild voice—"do you think you could find me some bread and butter? Or a glass of milk?"

Jane sat up in bed suddenly. She knew at once that she had made a mistake, but she was quite dignified about it. She looked over at the chair, and the convalescent typhoid was sitting in it, wrapped in a blanket and looking wan and ghostly in the dusk.

"I'm afraid I'm in the wrong room," Jane said very stiffly, trying to get out of the bed with dignity, which is difficult. "The hall is dark and all the doors look so alike— —"

She made for the door at that and got out into the hall with her heart going a thousand a minute again.

"You've forgotten your slippers," called the convalescent typhoid after her. But nothing would have taken Jane back.

The convalescent typhoid took the slippers home later and locked them away in an inner drawer, where he kept one or two things like faded roses, and old gloves, and a silk necktie that a girl had made him at college—things that are all the secrets a man keeps from his wife and that belong in that small corner of his heart which also he keeps from his wife. But that has nothing to do with Jane.

Jane went back to her own bed thoroughly demoralised. And sleep being pretty well banished by that time, she sat up in bed and thought things over. Before this she had not thought much, only raged and sulked alternately. But now she thought. She thought about the man in the room down the hall with the lines of dissipation on his face. And she thought a great deal about what a silly she had been, and that it was not too late yet, she being not forty and "beautiful." It must be confessed that she thought a great deal about that. Also she reflected that what she deserved was to marry some person with even a worse temper than hers, who would bully her at times and generally keep her straight. And from that, of course, it was only a step to the fact that red-haired people are proverbially bad-tempered!

She thought, too, about Mary O'Shaughnessy without another woman near, and not even a light, except perhaps a candle. Things were always so much worse in the darkness. And perhaps she might be going to be very ill and ought to have another doctor!

Jane seemed to have been reflecting for a long time, when the church clock far down in the village struck nine. And with the chiming of the clock was born, full grown, an idea which before it was sixty seconds of age was a determination.

In pursuance of the idea Jane once more crawled out of bed and began to dress; she put on heavy shoes and a short skirt, a coat, and a motor veil over her hair. The indignation at the defection of the hospital staff, held in subjection during the day by the necessity for doing something, now rose and lent speed and fury to her movements. In an incredibly short time Jane was feeling her way along the hall and down the staircase, now a well of unfathomable blackness and incredible rustlings and creakings.

The front doors were unlocked. Outside there was faint starlight, the chirp of a sleepy bird, and far off across the valley the gasping and wheezing of a freight climbing the heavy grade to the village.

Jane paused at the drive and took a breath. Then at her best gymnasium pace, arms close to sides, head up, feet well planted, she started to run. At the sundial she left the drive and took to the lawn gleaming with the frost of late October. She stopped running then and began to pick her way more cautiously. Even at that she collided heavily with a wire fence marking the boundary, and sat on the ground for some time after, whimpering over the outrage and feeling her nose. It was distinctly scratched and swollen. No one would think her beautiful with a nose like that!

She had not expected the wire fence. It was impossible to climb and more difficult to get under. However, she found one place where the ground dipped, and wormed her way under the fence in most undignified fashion. It is perfectly certain that had Jane's family seen her then and been told that she was doing this remarkable thing for a woman she had never seen before that day, named Mary O'Shaughnessy, and also for a certain red-haired person of whom it had never heard, it would have considered Jane quite irrational. But it is entirely probable that Jane became really rational that night for the first time in her spoiled young life.

Jane never told the details of that excursion. Those that came out in the paper were only guess-work, of course, but it is quite true that a reporter found scraps of her motor veil on three wire fences, and there seems to be no reason to doubt, also, that two false curls were discovered a week later in a cow pasture on her own estate. But as Jane never wore curls afterward anyhow ——

Well, Jane got to her own house about eleven and crept in like a thief to the telephone. There were more rustlings and creakings and rumblings in the empty house than she had ever imagined, and she went backward through the hall for fear of something coming after her. But, which is to the point, she got to the telephone and called up her father in the city.

The first message that astonished gentleman got was that a red-haired person at the hospital was very ill, having run into a wire fence and bruised a nose, and that he was to bring out at once from town two doctors, six nurses, a cook and a furnace man!

After a time, however, as Jane grew calmer, he got it straightened out, and said a number of things over the telephone anent the deserting staff that are quite forbidden by the rules both of the club and of the telephone company. He gave Jane full instructions about sending to the village and having somebody come up and stay with her, and about taking a hot footbath and going to bed between blankets, and when Jane replied meekly to everything "Yes, father," and "All right, father," he was so stunned by her mildness that he was certain she must be really ill.

Not that Jane had any idea of doing all these things. She hung up the telephone and gathered all the candles from all the candlesticks on the lower floor, and started back for the hospital. The moon had come up and she had no more trouble with fencing, but she was desperately tired. She climbed the drive slowly, coming to frequent pauses. The hospital, long and low and sleeping, lay before her, and in one upper window there was a small yellow light.

Jane climbed the steps and sat down on the top one. She felt very tired and sad and dejected, and she sat down on the upper step to think of how useless she was, and how much a man must know to be a doctor, and that perhaps she would take up nursing in earnest and amount to something, and — —

It was about three o'clock in the morning when the red-haired person, coming down belatedly to close the front doors, saw a shapeless heap on the porch surrounded by a radius of white-wax candles, and going up shoved at it with his foot. Whereat the heap moved slightly and muttered "Lemme shleep."

The red-haired person said "Good Heavens!" and bending down held a lighted match to the sleeper's face and stared, petrified. Jane opened her eyes, sat up and put her hand over her mutilated nose with one gesture.

"You!" said the red-haired person. And then mercifully the match went out.

"Don't light another," said Jane. "I'm an alarming sight. Would — would you mind feeling if my nose is broken?"

He didn't move to examine it. He just kept on kneeling and staring.

"Where have you been?" he demanded.

"Over to telephone," said Jane, and yawned. "They're bringing everybody in automobiles — doctors, nurses, furnace man — oh, dear me, I hope I mentioned a cook!"

"Do you mean to say," said the red-haired person wonderingly, "that you went by yourself across the fields and telephoned to get me out of this mess?"

"Not at all," Jane corrected him coolly. "I'm in the mess myself."

"You'll be ill again."

"I never was ill," said Jane. "I was here for a mean disposition."

Jane sat in the moonlight with her hands in her lap and looked at him calmly. The red-haired person reached over and took both her hands.

"You're a heroine," he said, and bending down he kissed first one and then the other. "Isn't it bad enough that you are beautiful without your also being brave?"

Jane eyed him, but he was in deadly earnest. In the moonlight his hair was really not red at all, and he looked pale and very, very tired. Something inside of Jane gave a curious thrill that was half pain. Perhaps it was the dying of her temper, perhaps — —

"Am I still beautiful with this nose?" she asked.

"You are everything that a woman should be," he said, and dropping her hands he got up. He stood there in the moonlight, straight and young and crowned with despair, and Jane looked up from under her long lashes.

"Then why don't you stay where you were?" she asked.

At that he reached down and took her hands again and pulled her to her feet. He was very strong.

"Because if I do I'll never leave you again," he said. "And I must go."

He dropped her hands, or tried to, but Jane wasn't ready to be dropped.

"You know," she said, "I've told you I'm a sulky, bad-tempered — —"

But at that he laughed suddenly, triumphantly, and put both his arms round her and held her close.

"I love you," he said, "and if you are bad-tempered, so am I, only I think I'm worse. It's a shame to spoil two houses with us, isn't it?"

To her eternal shame be it told, Jane never struggled. She simply held up her mouth to be kissed.

That is really all the story. Jane's father came with three automobiles that morning at dawn, bringing with him all that goes to make up a hospital, from a pharmacy clerk to absorbent cotton, and having left the new supplies in the office he stamped upstairs to Jane's room and flung open the door.

He expected to find Jane in hysterics and the pink silk kimono.

What he really saw was this: A coal fire was lighted in Jane's grate, and in a low chair before it, with her nose swollen level with her forehead, sat Jane, holding on her lap Mary O'Shaughnessy's baby, very new and magenta-coloured and yelling like a trooper. Kneeling beside the chair was a tall, red-headed person holding a bottle of olive oil.

"Now, sweetest," the red-haired person was saying, "turn him on his tummy and we'll rub his back. Gee, isn't that a fat back!"

And as Jane's father stared and Jane anxiously turned the baby, the red-haired person leaned over and kissed the back of Jane's neck.

"Jane!" he whispered.

"Jane!!" said her father.

IN THE PAVILION

I

Now, had Billy Grant really died there would be no story. The story is to relate how he nearly died; and how, approaching that bourne to which no traveller may take with him anything but his sins—and this with Billy Grant meant considerable luggage—he cast about for some way to prevent the Lindley Grants from getting possession of his worldly goods.

Probably it would never have happened at all had not young Grant, having hit on a scheme, clung to it with a tenacity that might better have been devoted to saving his soul, and had he not said to the Nurse, who was at that moment shaking a thermometer: "Come on—be a sport! It's only a matter of hours." Not that he said it aloud—he whispered it, and fought for the breath to do even that. The Nurse, having shaken down the thermometer, walked to the table and recorded a temperature of one hundred and six degrees through a most unprofessional mist of tears. Then in the symptom column she wrote: "Delirious."

But Billy Grant was not delirious. A fever of a hundred and four or thereabout may fuse one's mind in a sort of fiery crucible, but when it gets to a hundred and six all the foreign thoughts, like seeing green monkeys on the footboard and wondering why the doctor is walking on his hands—all these things melt away, and one sees one's past, as when drowning, and remembers to hate one's relations, and is curious about what is coming when one goes over.

So Billy Grant lay on his bed in the contagious pavilion of the hospital, and remembered to hate the Lindley Grants and to try to devise a way to keep them out of his property. And, having studied law, he knew no will that he might make now would hold against the Lindley Grants for a minute, unless he survived its making some thirty days. The Staff Doctor had given him about thirty hours or less.

Perhaps he would have given up in despair and been forced to rest content with a threat to haunt the Lindley Grants and otherwise mar the enjoyment of their good fortune, had not the Nurse at that moment put the thermometer under his arm.

Now, as every one knows, an axillary temperature takes five minutes, during which it is customary for a nurse to kneel beside the bed, or even to sit very lightly on the edge, holding the patient's arm close to his side and counting his respirations while pretending to be thinking of something else. It was during these five minutes that the idea came into Billy Grant's mind and, having come, remained. The Nurse got up, rustling starchily, and Billy caught her eye.

"Every engine," he said with difficulty, "labours—in a low—gear. No wonder I'm—heated up!"

The Nurse, who was young, put her hand on his forehead.

"Try to sleep," she said.

"Time for—that—later," said Billy Grant. "I'll—I'll be a—long time—dead. I—I wonder whether you'd—do me a—favour."

"I'll do anything in the world you want."

She tried to smile down at him, but only succeeded in making her chin quiver, which would never do—being unprofessional and likely to get to the head nurse; so, being obliged to do something, she took his pulse by the throbbing in his neck.

"One, two, three, four, five, six— —"

"Then—marry me," gasped Billy Grant. "Only for an—hour or—two, you know. You—promised. Come on—be a sport!"

It was then that the Nurse walked to the table and recorded "Delirious" in the symptom column. And, though she was a Smith College girl and had taken a something or other in mathematics, she spelled it just then with two r's.

Billy Grant was not in love with the Nurse. She was a part of his illness, like the narrow brass bed and the yellow painted walls, and the thermometer under his arm, and the medicines. There were even times—when his fever subsided for a degree or two, after a cold sponge, and the muddled condition of mind returned—when she seemed to have more heads than even a nurse requires. So sentiment did not enter into the matter at all; it was revenge.

"You—promised," he said again; but the Nurse only smiled indulgently and rearranged the bottles on the stand in neat rows.

Jenks, the orderly, carried her supper to the isolation pavilion at six o'clock—cold ham, potato salad, egg custard and tea. Also, he brought her an evening paper. But the Nurse was not hungry. She went into the bathroom, washed her eyes with cold water, put on a clean collar, against the impending visit of the Staff Doctor, and then stood at the window, looking across at the hospital and feeling very lonely and responsible. It was not a great hospital, but it loomed large and terrible that night. The ambulance came out into the courtyard, and an interne, in white ducks, came out to it, carrying a surgical bag. He looked over at her and waved his hand. "Big railroad wreck!" he called cheerfully. "Got 'em coming in bunches." He crawled into the ambulance, where the driver, trained to many internes, gave him time to light a cigarette; then out into the dusk, with the gong beating madly. Billy Grant, who had lapsed into a doze, opened his eyes.

"What—about it?" he asked. "You're not—married already—are you?"

"Please try to rest. Perhaps if I get your beef juice——"

"Oh, damn—the beef juice!" whispered Billy Grant, and shut his eyes again—but not to sleep. He was planning how to get his way, and finally, out of a curious and fantastic medley of thoughts, he evolved something. The doctor, of course! These women had to do what the doctor ordered. He would see the doctor! — upon which, with a precision quite amazing, all the green monkeys on the footboard of the bed put their thumbs to their noses at him.

The situation was unusual; for here was young Grant, far enough from any one who knew he was one of the Van Kleek Grants — and, as such, entitled to all the nurses and doctors that money could procure — shut away in the isolation pavilion of a hospital, and not even putting up a good fight! Even the Nurse felt this, and when the Staff Man came across the courtyard that night she met him on the doorstep and told him.

"He doesn't care whether he gets well or not," she said dispiritedly. "All he seems to think about is to die and to leave everything he owns so his relatives won't get it. It's horrible!"

The Staff Man, who had finished up a hard day with a hospital supper of steak and fried potatoes, sat down on the doorstep and fished out a digestive tablet from his surgical bag.

"It's pretty sad, little girl," he said, over the pill. He had known the Nurse for some time, having, in fact, brought her — according to report at the time — in a predecessor of the very bag at his feet, and he had the fatherly manner that belongs by right to the man who has first thumped one between the shoulder-blades to make one breathe, and who had remarked on this occasion to some one beyond the door: "A girl, and fat as butter!"

The Nurse tiptoed in and found Billy Grant apparently asleep. Actually he had only closed his eyes, hoping to lure one of the monkeys within clutching distance. So the Nurse came out again, with the symptom record.

"Delirious, with two r's," said the Staff Doctor, glancing over his spectacles. "He must have been pretty bad."

"Not wild; he — he wanted me to marry him!"

She smiled, showing a most alluring dimple in one cheek.

"I see! Well, that's not necessarily delirium. H'm — pulse, respiration — look at that temperature! Yes, it's pretty sad — away from home, too, poor lad!"

"You — — Isn't there any hope, doctor?"

"None at all — at least, I've never had 'em get well."

Now the Nurse should, by all the ethics of hospital practice, have walked behind the Staff Doctor, listening reverentially to what he said, not speaking until she was spoken to, and carrying in one hand an order blank on which said august personage would presently inscribe certain cabalistic characters, to be deciphered later by the pharmacy clerk with a strong light and much blasphemy, and in the other hand a clean towel. The clean towel does not enter into the story, but for the curious be it said that were said personage to desire to listen to the patient's heart, the towel would be unfolded and spread, without creases, over the patient's chest — which reminds me of the Irishman and the weary practitioner; but every one knows that story.

Now that is what the Nurse should have done; instead of which, in the darkened passageway, being very tired and exhausted and under a hideous strain, she suddenly slipped her arm through the Staff Doctor's and, putting her head on his shoulder, began to cry softly.

"What's this?" demanded the Staff Doctor sternly and, putting his arm round her: "Don't you know that Junior Nurses are not supposed to weep over the Staff?" And, getting no answer but a choke: "We can't have you used up like this; I'll make them relieve you. When did you sleep?"

"I don't want to be relieved," said the Nurse, very muffled. "No-nobody else would know wh-what he wanted. I just — I just can't bear to see him — to see him — —"

The Staff Doctor picked up the clean towel, which belonged on the Nurse's left arm, and dried her eyes for her; then he sighed.

"None of us likes to see it, girl," he said. "I'm an old man, and I've never got used to it. What do they send you to eat?"

"The food's all right," she said rather drearily. "I'm not hungry — that's all. How long do you think — — "

The Staff Doctor, who was putting an antiseptic gauze cap over his white hair, ran a safety pin into his scalp at that moment and did not reply at once. Then, "Perhaps — until morning," he said.

He held out his arms for the long, white, sterilised coat, and a moment later, with his face clean-washed of emotion, and looking like a benevolent Turk, he entered the sick room. The Nurse was just behind him, with an order book in one hand and a clean towel over her arm.

Billy Grant, from his bed, gave the turban a high sign of greeting.

"Allah — is — great!" he gasped cheerfully. "Well, doctor — I guess it's all — over but — the shouting."

II

Some time after midnight Billy Grant roused out of a stupor. He was quite rational; in fact, he thought he would get out of bed. But his feet would not move. This was absurd! One's feet must move if one wills them to! However, he could not stir either of them. Otherwise he was beautifully comfortable.

Faint as was the stir he made the Nurse heard him. She was sitting in the dark by the window.

"Water?" she asked softly, coming to him.

"Please." His voice was stronger than it had been.

Some of the water went down his neck, but it did not matter. Nothing mattered except the Lindley Grants. The Nurse took his temperature and went out into the hall to read the thermometer, so he might not watch her face. Then, having recorded it under the nightlight, she came back into the room.

"Why don't you put on something comfortable?" demanded Billy Grant querulously. He was so comfortable himself and she was so stiffly starched, so relentless of collar and cap.

"I am comfortable."

"Where's that wrapper thing you've been wearing at night?" The Nurse rather flushed at this. "Why don't you lie down on the cot and take a nap? I don't need anything."

"Not—not to-night."

He understood, of course, but he refused to be depressed. He was too comfortable. He was breathing easily, and his voice, though weak, was clear.

"Would you mind sitting beside me? Or are you tired? But of course you are. Perhaps in a night or so you'll be over there again, sleeping in a nice white gown in a nice fresh bed, with no querulous devil——"

"Please!"

"You'll have to be sterilised or formaldehyded?"

"Yes." This very low.

"Will you put your hand over mine? Thanks. It's—company, you know." He was apologetic; under her hand his own burned fire. "I—I spoke to the Staff about that while you were out of the room."

"About what?"

"About your marrying me."

"What did he say?" She humoured him.

"He said he was willing if you were. You're not going to move—are you?"

"No. But you must not talk."

"It's like this. I've got a little property—not much; a little." He was nervously eager about this. If she knew it amounted to anything she would refuse, and the Lindley Grants—— "And when I—you know—— I want to leave it where it will do some good. That little brother of yours—it would send him through college, or help to."

Once, weeks ago, before he became so ill, she had told him of the brother. This in itself was wrong and against the ethics of the profession. One does not speak of oneself or one's family.

"If you won't try to sleep, shall I read to you?"

"Read what?"

"I thought—the Bible, if you wouldn't mind."

"Certainly," he agreed. "I suppose that's the conventional thing; and if it makes you feel any better — — Will you think over what I've been saying?"

"I'll think about it," she said, soothing him like a fretful child, and brought her Bible.

The clock on the near-by town hall struck two as she drew up her chair beside him and commenced to read by the shaded light. Across the courtyard the windows were dim yellowish rectangles, with here and there one brighter than the others that told its own story of sleepless hours. A taxicab rolled along the street outside, carrying a boisterous night party.

The Nurse had taken off her cap and put it on a stand. The autumn night was warm, and the light touch of the tulle had pressed her hair in damp, fine curves over her forehead. There were purple hollows of anxiety and sleeplessness under her eyes.

"The perfect nurse," the head of the training school was fond of saying, "is more or less of a machine. Too much sympathy is a handicap to her work and an embarrassment to her patient. A perfect, silent, reliable, fearless, emotionless machine!"

Poor Junior Nurse!

Now Billy Grant, lying there listening to something out of Isaiah, should have been repenting his hard-living, hard-drinking young life; should have been forgiving the Lindley Grants—which story does not belong here; should have been asking for the consolation of the church, and trying to summon from the depths of his consciousness faint memories of early teachings as to the life beyond, and what he might or might not expect there.

What he actually did while the Nurse read was to try to move his legs, and, failing this, to plan a way to achieve the final revenge of a not particularly forgiving life.

At a little before three o'clock the Nurse telephoned across for an interne, who came over in a bathrobe over his pajamas and shot a hypodermic into Billy Grant's left arm. Billy Grant hardly noticed. He was seeing Mrs. Lindley Grant when his surprise was sprung on her. The interne summoned the Nurse into the hall with a jerk of his head.

"About all in!" he said. "Heart's gone — too much booze probably. I'd stay, but there's nothing to do."

"Would oxygen — —"

"Oh, you can try it if you like. It's like blowing up a leaking tire; but if you'll feel better, do it." He yawned and tied the cord of his bathrobe round him more securely. "I guess you'll be glad to get back," he observed, looking round the dingy hall. "This place always gives me a chill. Well, let me know if you want me. Good night."

The Nurse stood in the hallway until the echo of his slippers on the asphalt had died away. Then she turned to Billy Grant.

"Well?" demanded Billy Grant. "How long have I? Until morning?"

"If you would only not talk and excite yourself — —"

"Hell!" said Billy Grant, we regret to record. "I've got to do all the talking I'm going to do right now. I beg your pardon — I didn't intend to swear."

"Oh, that's all right!" said the Nurse vaguely. This was like no deathbed she had ever seen, and it was disconcerting.

"Shall I read again?"

"No, thank you."

The Nurse looked at her watch, which had been graduation present from her mother and which said, inside the case: "To my little girl!" There is no question but that, when the Nurse's mother gave that inscription to the jeweller, she was thinking of the day when the Staff Doctor had brought the Nurse in his leather bag, and had slapped her between the shoulders to make her breathe. "To my little girl!" said the watch; and across from that—"Three o'clock."

At half-past three Billy Grant, having matured his plans, remarked that if it would ease the Nurse any he'd see a preacher. His voice was weaker again and broken.

"Not"—he said, struggling—"not that I think—he'll pass me. But—if you say so—I'll—take a chance."

All of which was diabolical cunning; for when, as the result of a telephone conversation, the minister came, an unworldly man who counted the world, an automobile, a vested choir and a silver communion service well lost for the sake of a dozen derelicts in a slum mission house, Billy Grant sent the Nurse out to prepare a broth he could no longer swallow, and proceeded to cajole the man of God. This he did by urging the need of the Nurse's small brother for an education and by forgetting to mention either the Lindley Grants or the extent of his property.

From four o'clock until five Billy Grant coaxed the Nurse with what voice he had. The idea had become an obsession; and minute by minute, panting breath by panting breath, her resolution wore away. He was not delirious; he was as sane as she was and terribly set. And this thing he wanted was so easy to grant; meant so little to her and, for some strange reason, so much to him. Perhaps, if she did it, he would think a little of what the preacher was saying.

At five o'clock, utterly worn out with the struggle and finding his pulse a negligible quantity, in response to his pleading eyes the Nurse, kneeling and holding a thermometer under her patient's arm with one hand, reached the other one over the bed and was married in a dozen words and a soiled white apron.

Dawn was creeping in at the windows—a grey city dawn, filled with soot and the rumbling of early wagons. A smell of damp asphalt from the courtyard floated in and a dirty sparrow chirped on the sill where the Nurse had been in the habit of leaving crumbs. Billy Grant, very sleepy and contented now that he had got his way, dictated a line or two on a blank symptom record, and signed his will in a sprawling hand.

"If only," he muttered, "I could see Lin's face when that's—sprung on him!"

The minister picked up the Bible from the tumbled bed and opened it.

"Perhaps," he suggested very softly, "if I read from the Word of God——"

Satisfied now that he had fooled the Lindley Grants out of their very shoebuttons, Billy Grant was asleep—asleep with the thermometer under his arm and with his chest rising and falling peacefully.

The minister looked across at the Nurse, who was still holding the thermometer in place. She had buried her face in the white counterpane.

"You are a good woman, sister," he said softly. "The boy is happier, and you are none the worse. Shall I keep the paper for you?"

But the Nurse, worn out with the long night, slept where she knelt. The minister, who had come across the street in a ragged smoking-coat and no collar, creaked round the bed and threw the edge of the blanket over her shoulders.

Then, turning his coat collar up over his unshaved neck, he departed for the mission across the street, where one of his derelicts, in his shirtsleeves, was sweeping the pavement. There, mindful of the fact that he had come from the contagious pavilion, the minister brushed his shabby smoking-coat with a whiskbroom to remove the germs!

III

Billy Grant, of course, did not die. This was perhaps because only the good die young. And Billy Grant's creed had been the honour of a gentleman rather than the Mosaic Law. There was, therefore, no particular violence done to his code when his last thoughts — or what appeared to be his last thoughts — were revenge instead of salvation.

The fact was, Billy Grant had a real reason for hating the Lindley Grants. When a fellow like that has all the Van Kleek money and a hereditary thirst, he is bound to drink. The Lindley Grants did not understand this and made themselves obnoxious by calling him "Poor Billy!" and not having wine when he came to dinner. That, however, was not his reason for hating them.

Billy Grant fell in love. To give the devil his due, he promptly set about reforming himself. He took about half as many whisky-and-sodas as he had been in the habit of doing, and cut out champagne altogether. He took up golf to fill in the time, too, but gave it up when he found it made him thirstier than ever. And then, with things so shaping up that he could rise in the morning without having a drink to get up on, the Lindley Grants thought it best to warn the girl's family before it was too late.

"He is a nice boy in some ways," Mrs. Lindley Grant had said on the occasion of the warning; "but, like all drinking men, he is a broken reed, eccentric and irresponsible. No daughter of mine could marry him. I'd rather bury her. And if you want facts Lindley will give them to you."

So the girl had sent back her ring and a cold little letter, and Billy Grant had got roaring full at a club that night and presented the ring to a cabman — all of which is exceedingly sordid, but rather human after all.

The Nurse, having had no sleep for forty-eight hours, slept for quite thirty minutes. She wakened at the end of that time and started up with a horrible fear that the thing she was waiting for had come. But Billy Grant was still alive, sleeping naturally, and the thermometer, having been in place forty minutes, registered a hundred and three.

At eight o'clock the interne, hurrying over in fresh ducks, with a laudable desire to make the rounds before the Staff began to drop in, found Billy Grant very still and with his eyes closed, and the Nurse standing beside the bed, pale and tremulous.

"Why didn't you let me know?" he demanded, aggrieved. "I ought to have been called. I told you — — "

"He isn't dead," said the Nurse breathlessly. "He — I think he is better."

Whereon she stumbled out of the room into her own little room across the hall, locking the door behind her, and leaving the interne to hunt the symptom record for himself — a thing not to be lightly overlooked; though of course internes are not the Staff.

The interne looked over the record and whistled.

"Wouldn't that paralyse you!" he said under his breath. "'Pulse very weak.' 'Pulse almost obliterated.' 'Very talkative.' 'Breathing hard at four A.M. Cannot swallow.' And then: 'Sleeping calmly from five o'clock.' 'Pulse stronger.' Temperature one hundred and three.' By gad, that last prescription of mine was a hit!"

So now began a curious drama of convalescence in the little isolation pavilion across the courtyard. Not for a minute did the two people most concerned forget their strange relationship; not for worlds would either have allowed the other to know that he or she remembered. Now and then the Nurse caught Billy Grant's eyes fixed on her as she moved about the room, with a curious wistful expression in them. And sometimes, waking from a doze, he would find her in her chair by the window, with her book dropped into her lap and a frightened look in her eyes, staring at him.

He gained strength rapidly and the day came when, with the orderly's assistance, he was lifted to a chair. There was one brief moment in which he stood tottering on his feet. In that instant he had realised what a little thing she was, after all, and what a cruel advantage he had used for his own purpose.

When he was settled in the chair and the orderly had gone she brought an extra pillow to put behind him, and he dared the first personality of their new relationship.

"What a little girl you are, after all!" he said. "Lying there in the bed shaking at your frown, you were so formidable."

"I am not small," she said, straightening herself. She had always hoped that her cap gave her height. "It is you who are so tall. You — you are a giant!"

"A wicked giant, seeking whom I may devour and carrying off lovely girls for dinner under pretence of marriage — —" He stopped his nonsense abruptly, having got so far, and both of them coloured. Thrashing about desperately for something to break the wretched silence, he seized on the one thing that in those days of his convalescence was always pertinent — food. "Speaking of dinner," he said hastily, "isn't it time for some buttermilk?"

She was quite calm when she came back — cool, even smiling; but Billy Grant had not had the safety valve of action. As she placed the glass on the table at his elbow he reached out and took her hand.

"Can you ever forgive me?" he asked. Not an original speech; the usual question of the marauding male, a query after the fact and too late for anything but forgiveness.

"Forgive you? For not dying?"

She was pale; but no more subterfuge now, no more turning aside from dangerous subjects. The matter was up before the house.

"For marrying you!" said Billy Grant, and upset the buttermilk. It took a little time to wipe up the floor and to put a clean cover on the stand, and after that to bring a fresh glass and place it on the table. But these were merely parliamentary preliminaries while each side got its forces in line.

"Do you hate me very much?" opened Billy Grant. This was, to change the figure, a blow below the belt.

"Why should I hate you?" countered the other side.

"I should think you would. I forced the thing on you."

"I need not have done it."

"But being you, and always thinking about making some one else happy and comfortable——"

"Oh, if only they don't find it out over there!" she burst out. "If they do and I have to leave, with Jim——"

Here, realising that she was going to cry and not caring to screw up her face before any one, she put her arms on the stand and buried her face in them. Her stiff tulle cap almost touched Billy Grant's arm.

Billy Grant had a shocked second.

"Jim?"

"My little brother," from the table.

Billy Grant drew a long breath of relief. For a moment he had thought——

"I wonder—whether I dare to say something to you." Silence from the table and presumably consent. "Isn't he—don't you think that—I might be allowed to—to help Jim? It would help me to like myself again. Just now I'm not standing very high with myself."

"Won't you tell me why you did it?" she said, suddenly sitting up, her arms still out before her on the table. "Why did you coax so? You said it was because of a little property you had, but—that wasn't it—was it?"

"No."

"Or because you cared a snap for me." This was affirmation, not question.

"No, not that, though I——"

She gave a hopeless little gesture of despair.

"Then—why? Why?"

"For one of the meanest reasons I know—to be even with some people who had treated me badly."

The thing was easier now. His flat denial of any sentimental reason had helped to make it so.

"A girl that you cared about?"

"Partly that. The girl was a poor thing. She didn't care enough to be hurt by anything I did. But the people who made the trouble——"

Now a curious thing happened. Billy Grant found at this moment that he no longer hated the Lindley Grants. The discovery left him speechless—that he who had taken his hate into the very valley of death with him should now find himself thinking of both Lindley and his wife with nothing more bitter than contempt shocked him. A state of affairs existed for which his hatred of the Lindley Grants was alone responsible; now the hate was gone and the state of affairs persisted.

"I should like," said Billy Grant presently, "to tell you a little—if it will not bore you—about myself and the things I have done that I shouldn't, and about the girl. And of course, you know, I'm—I'm not going to hold you to—to the thing I forced you into. There are ways to fix that."

Before she would listen, however, she must take his temperature and give him his medicine, and see that he drank his buttermilk—the buttermilk last, so as not to chill his mouth for the thermometer. The tired lines had gone from under her eyes and she was very lovely that day. She had always been lovely, even when the Staff Doctor had slapped her between the shoulders long ago—you know about that—only Billy Grant had never noticed it; but to-day, sitting there with the thermometer in his mouth while she counted his respirations, pretending to be looking out the window while she did it, Billy Grant saw how sweet and lovely and in every way adorable she was, in spite of the sad droop of her lips—and found it hard to say the thing he felt he must.

"After all," he remarked round the thermometer, "the thing is not irrevocable. I can fix it up so that——"

"Keep your lips closed about the thermometer!" she said sternly, and snapped her watch shut.

The pulse and so on having been recorded, and "Very hungry" put down under Symptoms, she came back to her chair by the window, facing him. She sat down primly and smoothed her white apron in her lap.

"Now!" she said.

"I am to go on?"

"Yes, please."

"If you are going to change the pillows or the screen, or give me any other diabolical truck to swallow," he said somewhat peevishly, "will you get it over now, so we can have five unprofessional minutes?"

"Certainly," she said; and bringing an extra blanket she spread it, to his disgust, over his knees.

This time, when she sat down, one of her hands lay on the table near him and he reached over and covered it with his.

"Please!" he begged. "For company! And it will help me to tell you some of the things I have to tell."

She left it there, after an uneasy stirring. So, sitting there, looking out into the dusty courtyard with its bandaged figures in wheeled chairs, its cripples sunning on a bench—their crutches beside them—its waterless fountain and its dingy birds, he told her about the girl and the Lindley Grants, and even about the cabman and the ring. And feeling, perhaps in some current from the small hand under his, that she was knowing and understanding and not turning away, he told her a great deal he had not meant to tell—ugly things, many of them—for that was his creed.

And, because in a hospital one lives many lives vicariously with many people, what the girl back home would never have understood this girl did and faced unabashed. Life, as she knew it, was not all good and not all bad; passion and tenderness, violence and peace, joy and wretchedness, birth and death—these she had looked on, all of them, with clear eyes and hands ready to help.

So Billy Grant laid the good and the bad of his life before her, knowing that he was burying it with her. When he finished, her hand on the table had turned and was clasping his. He bent over and kissed her fingers softly.

After that she read to him, and their talk, if any, was impersonal. When the orderly had put him back to bed he lay watching her moving about, rejoicing in her quiet strength, her repose. How well she was taking it all! If only—but there was no hope of that. She could go to Reno, and in a few months she would be free again and the thing would be as if it had never been.

At nine o'clock that night the isolation pavilion was ready for the night. The lights in the sickroom were out. In the hall a nightlight burned low, Billy Grant was not asleep. He tried counting the lighted windows of the hospital and grew only more wakeful.

The Nurse was sleeping now in her own room across, with the doors open between. The slightest movement and she was up, tiptoeing in, with her hair in a long braid down her back and her wrapper sleeves falling away loosely from her white, young arms. So, aching with inaction, Billy Grant lay still until the silence across indicated that she was sleeping.

Then he got up. This is a matter of difficulty when one is still very weak, and is achieved by rising first into a sitting posture by pulling oneself up by the bars of the bed, and then by slipping first one leg, then the other, over the side. Properly done, even the weakest thus find themselves in a position that by the aid of a chairback may become, however shaky, a standing one.

He got to his feet better than he expected, but not well enough to relinquish the chair. He had made no sound. That was good. He would tell her in the morning and rally her on her powers as a sleeper. He took a step—if only his knees——

He had advanced into line with the doorway and stood looking through the open door of the room across.

The Nurse was on her knees beside the bed, in her nightgown, crying. Her whole young body was shaken with silent sobs; her arms, in their short white sleeves, stretched across the bed, her fingers clutching the counterpane.

Billy Grant stumbled back to his bed and fell in with a sort of groan. Almost instantly she was at the door, her flannel wrapper held about her, peering into the darkness.

"I thought I heard—are you worse?" she asked anxiously.

"I'm all right," he said, hating himself; "just not sleepy. How about you?"

"Not asleep yet, but—resting," she replied.

She stood in the doorway, dimly outlined, with her long braid over her shoulder and her voice still a little strained from crying. In the darkness Billy Grant half stretched out his arms, then dropped them, ashamed.

"Would you like another blanket?"

"If there is one near."

She came in a moment later with the blanket and spread it over the bed. He lay very still while she patted and smoothed it into place. He was mustering up his courage to ask for something—a curious state of mind for Billy Grant, who had always taken what he wanted without asking.

"I wish you would kiss me—just once!" he said wistfully. And then, seeing her draw back, he took an unfair advantage: "I think that's the reason I'm not sleeping."

"Don't be absurd!"

"Is it so absurd—under the circumstances?"

"You can sleep quite well if you only try."

She went out into the hall again, her chin well up. Then she hesitated, turned and came swiftly back into the room.

"If I do," she said rather breathlessly, "will you go to sleep? And will you promise to hold your arms up over your head?"

"But my arms— —"

"Over your head!"

He obeyed at that, and the next moment she had bent over him in the darkness; and quickly, lightly, deliciously, she kissed—the tip of his nose!

IV

She was quite cheerful the next day and entirely composed. Neither of them referred to the episode of the night before, but Billy Grant thought of little else. Early in the morning he asked her to bring him a hand mirror and, surveying his face, tortured and disfigured by the orderly's shaving, suffered an acute wound in his vanity. He was glad it had been dark or she probably would not have— — He borrowed a razor from the interne and proceeded to enjoy himself.

Propped up in his chair, he rioted in lather, sliced a piece out of his right ear, and shaved the back of his neck by touch, in lieu of better treatment. This done, and the ragged and unkempt hair over his ears having been trimmed in scallops, due to the work being done with curved surgical scissors, he was his own man again.

That afternoon, however, he was nervous and restless. The Nurse was troubled. He avoided the subject that had so obsessed him the day before, was absent and irritable, could not eat, and sat in his chair by the window, nervously clasping and unclasping his hands.

The Nurse was puzzled, but the Staff Doctor, making rounds that day, enlightened her.

"He has pulled through—God and you alone know how," he said. "But as soon as he begins to get his strength he's going to yell for liquor again. When a man has been soaking up alcohol for years— — Drat this hospital cooking anyhow! Have you got any essence of pepsin?"

The Nurse brought the pepsin and a medicine glass and the Staff Doctor swallowed and grimaced.

"You were saying," said the Nurse timidly—for, the stress being over, he was Staff again and she was a Junior and not even entitled to a Senior's privileges, such as returning occasional badinage.

"Every atom of him is going to crave it. He's wanting it now. He has been used to it for years." The Nurse was white to the lips, but steady. "He is not to have it?"

"Not a drop while he is here. When he gets out it is his own affair again, but while he's here—by-the-way, you'll have to watch the orderly. He'll bribe him."

"I don't think so, doctor. He is a gentleman."

"Pooh! Of course he is. I dare say he's a gentleman when he's drunk too; but he's a drinker—a habitual drinker."

The Nurse went back into the room and found Billy Grant sitting in a chair, with the book he had been reading on the floor and his face buried in his hands.

"I'm awfuly sorry!" he said, not looking up. "I heard what he said. He's right, you know."

"I'm sorry. And I'm afraid this is a place where I cannot help."

She put her hand on his head, and he brought it down and held it between his.

"Two or three times," he said, "when things were very bad with me, you let me hold your hand, and we got past somehow—didn't we?"

She closed her eyes, remembering the dawn when, to soothe a dying man, in the presence of the mission preacher, she had put her hand in his. Billy Grant thought of it too.

"Now you know what you've married," he said bitterly. The bitterness was at himself of course. "If—if you'll sit tight I have a fighting chance to make a man of myself; and after it's over we'll fix this thing for you so you will forget it ever happened. And I— — Don't take your hand away. Please!"

"I was feeling for my handkerchief," she explained.

"Have I made you cry again?"

"Again?'

"I saw you last night in your room. I didn't intend to; but I was trying to stand, and——"

She was very dignified at this, with her eyes still wet, and tried unsuccessfully to take her hand away.

"If you are going to get up when it is forbidden I shall ask to be relieved."

"You wouldn't do that!"

"Let go of my hand."

"You wouldn't do that!!"

"Please! The head nurse is coming."

He freed her hand then and she wiped her eyes, remembering the "perfect, silent, reliable, fearless, emotionless machine."

The head of the training school came to the door of the pavilion, but did not enter. The reason for this was twofold: first, she had confidence in the Nurse; second, she was afraid of contagion—this latter, of course, quite sub rosa, in view of the above quotation.

The Head Nurse was a tall woman in white, and was so starchy that she rattled like a newspaper when she walked.

"Good morning," she said briskly. "Have you sent over the soiled clothes?" Head nurses are always bothering about soiled clothes; and what becomes of all the nailbrushes, and how can they use so many bandages.

"Yes, Miss Smith."

"Meals come over promptly?"

"Yes, Miss Smith."

"Getting any sleep?"

"Oh, yes, plenty—now."

Miss Smith peered into the hallway, which seemed tidy, looked at the Nurse with approval, and then from the doorstep into the patient's room, where Billy Grant sat. At the sight of him her eyebrows rose.

"Good gracious!" she exclaimed. "I thought he was older than that!"

"Twenty-nine," said the Nurse; "twenty-nine last Fourth of July."

"H'm!" commented the Head Nurse. "You evidently know! I had no idea you were taking care of a boy. It won't do. I'll send over Miss Hart."

The Nurse tried to visualise Billy Grant in his times of stress clutching at Miss Hart's hand, and failed.

"Jenks is here, of course," she said, Jenks being the orderly.

The idea of Jenks as a chaperon, however, did not appeal to the head nurse. She took another glance through the window at Billy Grant, looking uncommonly handsome and quite ten years younger since the shave, and she set her lips.

"I am astonished beyond measure," she said. "Miss Hart will relieve you at two o'clock. Take your antiseptic bath and you may have the afternoon to yourself. Report in L Ward in the morning."

Miss Smith rattled back across the courtyard and the Nurse stood watching her; then turned slowly and went into the house to tell Billy Grant.

Now the stories about what followed differ. They agree on one point: that Billy Grant had a heart-to-heart talk with the substitute at two o'clock that afternoon and told her politely but firmly that he would none of her. Here the divergence begins. Some say he got the superintendent over the house telephone and said he had intended to make a large gift to the hospital, but if his comfort was so little considered as to change nurses just when he had got used to one, he would have to alter his plans. Another and more likely story, because it sounds more like Billy Grant, is that at five o'clock a florist's boy delivered to Miss Smith a box of orchids such as never had been seen before in the house, and a card inside which said: "Please, dear Miss Smith, take back the Hart that thou gavest."

Whatever really happened — and only Billy Grant and the lady in question ever really knew — that night at eight o'clock, with Billy Grant sitting glumly in his room and Miss Hart studying typhoid fever in the hall, the Nurse came back again to the pavilion with her soft hair flying from its afternoon washing and her eyes shining. And things went on as before — not quite as before; for with the nurse question settled the craving got in its work again, and the next week was a bad one. There were good days, when he taught her double-dummy auction bridge, followed by terrible nights, when he walked the floor for hours and she sat by, unable to help. Then at dawn he would send her to bed remorsefully and take up the fight alone. And there were quiet nights when both slept and when he would waken to the craving again and fight all day.

"I'm afraid I'm about killing her," he said to the Staff Doctor one day; "but it's my chance to make a man of myself — now or never."

The Staff Doctor was no fool and he had heard about the orchids.

"Fight it out, boy!" he said. "Pretty soon you'll quit peeling and cease being a menace to the public health, and you'd better get it over before you are free again."

So, after a time, it grew a little easier. Grant was pretty much himself again — had put on a little flesh and could feel his biceps rise under his fingers. He took to cold plunges when he felt the craving coming on, and there were days when the little pavilion was full of the sound of running water. He shaved himself daily, too, and sent out for some collars.

Between the two of them, since her return, there had been much of good fellowship, nothing of sentiment. He wanted her near, but he did not put a hand on her. In the strain of those few days the strange, grey dawn seemed to have faded into its own mists. Only once, when she had brought his breakfast tray and was arranging the dishes for him—against his protest, for he disliked being waited on—he reached over and touched a plain band ring she wore. She coloured.

"My mother's," she said; "her wedding ring."

Their eyes met across the tray, but he only said, after a moment: "Eggs like a rock, of course! Couldn't we get 'em raw and boil them over here?"

It was that morning, also, that he suggested a thing which had been in his mind for some time.

"Wouldn't it be possible," he asked, "to bring your tray in here and to eat together? It would be more sociable."

She smiled.

"It isn't permitted."

"Do you think—would another box of orchids——"

She shook her head as she poured out his coffee. "I should probably be expelled."

He was greatly aggrieved.

"That's all foolishness," he said. "How is that any worse—any more unconventional—than your bringing me your extra blanket on a cold night? Oh, I heard you last night!"

"Then why didn't you leave it on?"

"And let you freeze?"

"I was quite warm. As it was, it lay in the hallway all night and did no one any good."

Having got thus far from wedding rings, he did not try to get back. He ate alone, and after breakfast, while she took her half-hour of exercise outside the window, he sat inside reading—only apparently reading, however.

Once she went quite as far as the gate and stood looking out.

"Jenks!" called Billy Grant.

Jenks has not entered into the story much. He was a little man, rather fat, who occupied a tiny room in the pavilion, carried meals and soiled clothes, had sat on Billy Grant's chest once or twice during a delirium, and kept a bottle locked in the dish closet.

"Yes, sir," said Jenks, coming behind a strong odour of spiritus frumenti.

"Jenks," said Billy Grant with an eye on the figure at the gate, "is that bottle of yours empty?"

"What bottle?"

"The one in the closet."

Jenks eyed Billy Grant, and Billy eyed Jenks—a look of man to man, brother to brother.

"Not quite, sir—a nip or two."

"At," suggested Billy Grant, "say—five dollars a nip?"

Jenks smiled.

"About that," he said. "Filled?"

Billy Grant debated. The Nurse was turning at the gate.

"No," he said. "As it is, Jenks. Bring it here."

Jenks brought the bottle and a glass, but the glass was motioned away. Billy Grant took the bottle in his hand and looked at it with a curious expression. Then he went over and put it in the upper bureau drawer, under a pile of handkerchiefs. Jenks watched him, bewildered.

"Just a little experiment, Jenks," said Billy Grant.

Jenks understood then and stopped smiling.

"I wouldn't, Mr. Grant," he said; "it will only make you lose confidence in yourself when it doesn't work out."

"But it's going to work out," said Billy Grant. "Would you mind turning on the cold water?"

Now the next twenty-four hours puzzled the Nurse. When Billy Grant's eyes were not on her with an unfathomable expression in them, they were fixed on something in the neighbourhood of the dresser, and at these times they had a curious, fixed look not unmixed with triumph. She tried a new arrangement of combs and brushes and tilted the mirror at a different angle, without effect.

That day Billy Grant took only one cold plunge. As the hours wore on he grew more cheerful; the look of triumph was unmistakable. He stared less at the dresser and more at the Nurse. At last it grew unendurable. She stopped in front of him and looked down at him severely. She could only be severe when he was sitting—when he was standing she had to look so far up at him, even when she stood on her tiptoes.

"What is wrong with me?" she demanded. "You look so queer! Is my cap crooked?"

"It is a wonderful cap."

"Is my face dirty?"

"It is a won— — No, certainly not."

"Then would you mind not staring so? You — upset me."

"I shall have to shut my eyes," he replied meekly, and worried her into a state of frenzy by sitting for fifty minutes with his head back and his eyes shut.

So — the evening and the morning were another day, and the bottle lay undisturbed under the handkerchiefs, and the cold shower ceased running, and Billy Grant assumed the air of triumph permanently. That morning when the breakfast trays came he walked over into the Nurse's room and picked hers up, table and all, carrying it across the hall. In his own room he arranged the two trays side by side, and two chairs opposite each other. When the Nurse, who had been putting breadcrumbs on the window-sill, turned round Billy Grant was waiting to draw out one of the chairs, and there was something in his face she had not seen there before.

"Shall we breakfast?" he said.

"I told you yesterday — —"

"Think a minute," he said softly. "Is there any reason why we should not breakfast together?" She pressed her hands close together, but she did not speak. "Unless — you do not wish to."

"You remember you promised, as soon as you got away, to — fix that — —"

"So I will if you say the word."

"And — to forget all about it."

"That," said Billy Grant solemnly, "I shall never do so long as I live. Do you say the word?"

"What else can I do?"

"Then there is somebody else?"

"Oh, no!"

He took a step toward her, but still he did not touch her.

"If there is no one else," he said, "and if I tell you that you have made me a man again — —"

"Gracious! Your eggs will be cold." She made a motion toward the egg-cup, but Billy Grant caught her hand.

"Damn the eggs!" he said. "Why don't you look at me?"

Something sweet and luminous and most unprofessional shone in the little Nurse's eyes, and the line of her pulse on a chart would have looked like a seismic disturbance.

"I — I have to look up so far!" she said, but really she was looking down when she said it.

"Oh, my dear — my dear!" exulted Billy Grant. "It is I who must look up at you!" And with that he dropped on his knees and kissed the starched hem of her apron.

The Nurse felt very absurd and a little frightened.

"If only," she said, backing off — "if only you wouldn't be such a silly! Jenks is coming!"

But Jenks was not coming. Billy Grant rose to his full height and looked down at her — a new Billy Grant, the one who had got drunk at a club and given a ring to a cabman having died that grey morning some weeks before.

"I love you — love you — love you!" he said, and took her in his arms.

Now the Head Nurse was interviewing an applicant; and, as the H.N. took a constitutional each morning in the courtyard and believed in losing no time, she was holding the interview as she walked.

"I think I would make a good nurse," said the applicant, a trifle breathless, the h.n. being a brisk walker. "I am so sympathetic."

The H.N. stopped and raised a reproving forefinger.

"Too much sympathy is a handicap," she orated. "The perfect nurse is a silent, reliable, fearless, emotionless machine—this little building here is the isolation pavilion."

"An emotionless machine," repeated the applicant. "I see—an e——"

The words died on her lips. She was looking past a crowd of birds on the windowsill to where, just inside, Billy Grant and the Nurse in a very mussed cap were breakfasting together. And as she looked Billy Grant bent over across the tray.

"I adore you!" he said distinctly and, lifting the Nurse's hands, kissed first one and then the other.

"It is hard work," said Miss Smith—having made a note that the boys in the children's ward must be restrained from lowering a pasteboard box on a string from a window—"hard work without sentiment. It is not a romantic occupation."

She waved an admonitory hand toward the window, and the box went up swiftly. The applicant looked again toward the pavilion, where Billy Grant, having kissed the Nurse's hands, had buried his face in her two palms.

The mild October sun shone down on the courtyard, with its bandaged figures in wheel-chairs, its cripples sunning on a bench, their crutches beside them, its waterless fountain and dingy birds.

The applicant thrilled to it all—joy and suffering, birth and death, misery and hope, life and love. Love!

The H.N. turned to her grimly, but her eyes were soft.

"All this," she said, waving her hand vaguely, "for eight dollars a month!"

GOD'S FOOL

I

The great God endows His children variously. To some He gives intellect—and they move the earth. To some He allots heart—and the beating pulse of humanity is theirs. But to some He gives only a soul, without intelligence—and these, who never grow up, but remain always His children, are God's fools, kindly, elemental, simple, as if from His palette the Artist of all had taken one colour instead of many.

The Dummy was God's fool. Having only a soul and no intelligence, he lived the life of the soul. Through his faded, childish old blue eyes he looked out on a world that hurried past him with, at best, a friendly touch on his shoulder. No man shook his hand in comradeship. No woman save the little old mother had ever caressed him. He lived alone in a world of his own fashioning, peopled by moving, noiseless figures and filled with dreams—noiseless because the Dummy had ears that heard not and lips that smiled at a kindness, but that did not speak.

In this world of his there was no uncharitableness—no sin. There was a God—why should he not know his Father?—there were brasses to clean and three meals a day; and there was chapel on Sunday, where one held a book—the Dummy held his upside down—and felt the vibration of the organ, and proudly watched the afternoon sunlight smiling on the polished metal of the chandelier and choir rail.

The Probationer sat turning the bandage machine and watching the Dummy, who was polishing the brass plates on the beds. The plates said: "Endowed in perpetuity"—by various leading citizens, to whom God had given His best gifts, both heart and brain.

"How old do you suppose he is?" she asked, dropping her voice.

The Senior Nurse was writing fresh labels for the medicine closet, and for "tincture of myrrh" she wrote absently "tincture of mirth," and had to tear it up.

"He can't hear you," she said rather shortly. "How old? Oh, I don't know. About a hundred, I should think."

This was, of course, because of his soul, which was all he had, and which, having existed from the beginning, was incredibly old. The little dead mother could have told them that he was less than thirty.

The Probationer sat winding bandages. Now and then they went crooked and had to be done again. She was very tired. The creaking of the bandage machine made her nervous — that and a sort of disillusionment; for was this her great mission, this sitting in a silent, sunny ward, where the double row of beds held only querulous convalescent women? How close was she to life who had come to soothe the suffering and close the eyes of the dying; who had imagined that her instruments of healing were a thermometer and a prayer-book; and who found herself fighting the good fight with a bandage machine and, even worse, a scrubbing brush and a finetooth comb?

The Senior Nurse, having finished the M's, glanced up and surprised a tear on the Probationer's round young cheek. She was wise, having trained many probationers.

"Go to first supper, please," she said. First supper is the Senior's prerogative; but it is given occasionally to juniors and probationers as a mark of approval, or when the Senior is not hungry, or when a probationer reaches the breaking point, which is just before she gets her uniform.

The Probationer smiled and brightened. After all, she must be doing fairly well; and if she were not in the battle she was of it. Glimpses she had of the battle — stretchers going up and down in the slow elevator; sheeted figures on their way to the operating room; the clang of the ambulance bell in the courtyard; the occasional cry of a new life ushered in; the impressive silence of an old life going out. She surveyed the bandages on the bed.

"I'll put away the bandages first," she said. "That's what you said, I think — never to leave the emergency bed with anything on it?"

"Right-oh!" said the Senior.

"Though nothing ever happens back here — does it?'

"It's about our turn; I'm looking for a burned case." The Probationer, putting the bandages into a basket, turned and stared.

"We have had two in to-day in the house," the Senior went on, starting on the N's and making the capital carefully. "There will be a third, of course; and we may get it. Cases always seem to run in threes. While you're straightening the bed I suppose I might as well go to supper after all."

So it was the Probationer and the Dummy who received the new case, while the Senior ate cold salmon and fried potatoes with other seniors, and inveighed against lectures on Saturday evening and other things that seniors object to, such as things lost in the wash, and milk in the coffee instead of cream, and women from the Avenue who drank carbolic acid and kept the ambulance busy.

The Probationer was from the country and she had never heard of the Avenue. And the Dummy, who walked there daily with the superintendent's dog, knew nothing of its wickedness. In his soul, where there was nothing but kindness, there was even a feeling of tenderness for the Avenue. Once the dog had been bitten by a terrier from one of the houses, and a girl had carried him in and washed the wounds and bound them up. Thereafter the Dummy had watched for her and bowed when he saw her. When he did not see her he bowed to the house.

The Dummy finished the brass plates and, gathering up his rags and polish, shuffled to the door. His walk was a patient shamble, but he covered incredible distances. When he reached the emergency bed he stopped and pointed to it. The Probationer looked startled.

"He's tellin' you to get it ready," shrilled Irish Delia, sitting up in the next bed. "He did that before you was brought in," she called to Old Maggie across the ward. "Goodness knows how he finds out—but he knows. Get the spread off the bed, miss. There's something coming."

The Probationer had come from the country and naturally knew nothing of the Avenue. Sometimes on her off duty she took short walks there, wondering if the passers-by who stared at her knew that she was a part of the great building that loomed over the district, happily ignorant of the real significance of their glances. Once a girl, sitting behind bowed shutters, had leaned out and smiled at her.

"Hot to-day, isn't it?" she said.

The Probationer stopped politely.

"It's fearful! Is there any place near where I can get some soda water?"

The girl in the window stared.

"There's a drug store two squares down," she said. "And say, if I were you——"

"Yes?"

"Oh, nothing!" said the girl in the window, and quite unexpectedly slammed the shutters.

The Probationer had puzzled over it quite a lot. More than once she walked by the house, but she did not see the smiling girl—only, curiously enough, one day she saw the Dummy passing the house and watched him bow and take off his old cap, though there was no one in sight.

Sooner or later the Avenue girls get to the hospital. Sometimes it is because they cannot sleep, and lie and think things over—and there is no way out;

and God hates them—though, of course, there is that story about Jesus and the Avenue woman. And what is the use of going home and being asked questions that cannot be answered? So they try to put an end to things generally—and end up in the emergency bed, terribly frightened, because it has occurred to them that if they do not dare to meet the home folks how are they going to meet the Almighty?

Or sometimes it is jealousy. Even an Avenue woman must love some one; and, because she's an elemental creature, if the object of her affections turns elsewhere she's rather apt to use a knife or a razor. In that case it is the rival who ends up on the emergency bed.

Or the life gets her, as it does sooner or later, and she comes in with typhoid or a cough, or other things, and lies alone, day after day, without visitors or inquiries, making no effort to get better, because—well, why should she?

And so the Dummy's Avenue Girl met her turn and rode down the street in a clanging ambulance, and was taken up in the elevator and along a grey hall to where the emergency bed was waiting; and the Probationer, very cold as to hands and feet, was sending mental appeals to the Senior to come—and come quickly. The ward got up on elbows and watched. Also it told the Probationer what to do.

"Hot-water bottles and screens," it said variously. "Take her temperature. Don't be frightened! There'll be a doctor in a minute."

The girl lay on the bed with her eyes shut. It was Irish Delia who saw the Dummy and raised a cry.

"Look at the Dummy!" she said. "He's crying."

The Dummy's world had always been a small one. There was the superintendent, who gave him his old clothes; and there was the engineer, who brought him tobacco; and there were the ambulance horses, who talked to him now and then without speech. And, of course, there was his Father.

Fringing this small inner circle of his heart was a kaleidoscope of changing faces, nurses, internes, patients, visitors—a wall of life that kept inviolate his inner shrine. And in the holiest place, where had dwelt only his Father, and not even the superintendent, the Dummy had recently placed the Avenue Girl. She was his saint, though he knew nothing of saints. Who can know why he chose her? A queer trick of the soul perhaps—or was it super-wisdom?—to choose her from among many saintly women and so enshrine her.

Or perhaps—— Down in the chapel, in a great glass window, the young John knelt among lilies and prayed. When, at service on Sundays, the sunlight came through on to the Dummy's polished choir rail and candles, the young John had the face of a girl, with short curling hair, very yellow for the colour scheme. The Avenue Girl had hair like that and was rather like him in other ways.

And here she was where all the others had come, and where countless others would come sooner or later. She was not unconscious and at Delia's cry she opened her eyes. The Probationer was off filling water bottles, and only the Dummy, stricken, round-shouldered, unlovely, stood beside her.

"Rotten luck, old top!" she said faintly.

To the Dummy it was a benediction. She could open her eyes. The miracle of speech was still hers.

"Cigarette!" explained the Avenue Girl, seeing his eyes still on her. "Must have gone to sleep with it and dropped it. I'm—all in!"

"Don't you talk like that," said Irish Delia, bending over from the next bed. "You'll get well a' right—unless you inhaled. Y'ought to 'a' kept your mouth shut."

Across the ward Old Maggie had donned her ragged slippers and a blue calico wrapper and shuffled to the foot of the emergency bed. Old Maggie was of that vague neighbourhood back of the Avenue, where squalor and poverty rubbed elbows with vice, and scorned it.

"Humph!" she said, without troubling to lower her voice. "I've seen her often. I done her washing once. She's as bad as they make 'em."

"You shut your mouth!" Irish Delia rose to the defence. "She's in trouble now and what she was don't matter. You go back to bed or I'll tell the Head Nurse on you. Look out! The Dummy——"

The Dummy was advancing on Old Maggie with threatening eyes. As the woman recoiled he caught her arm in one of his ugly, misshapen hands and jerked her away from the bed. Old Maggie reeled—almost fell.

"You all seen that!" she appealed to the ward. "I haven't even spoke to him and he attacked me! I'll go to the superintendent about it. I'll——"

The Probationer hurried in. Her young cheeks were flushed with excitement and anxiety; her arms were full of jugs, towels, bandages—anything she could imagine as essential. She found the Dummy on his knees polishing a bed plate, and the ward in order—only Old Maggie was grumbling and making her way back to bed; and Irish Delia was sitting up, with her eyes shining—for had not the Dummy, who could not hear, known what Old Maggie had said about the new girl? Had she not said that he knew many things that were hidden, though God knows how he knew them?

The next hour saw the Avenue Girl through a great deal. Her burns were dressed by an interne and she was moved back to a bed at the end of the ward. The Probationer sat beside her, having refused supper. The Dummy was gone—the Senior Nurse had shooed him off as one shoos a chicken.

"Get out of here! You're always under my feet," she had said—not unkindly—and pointed to the door.

The Dummy had stood, with his faded old-young eyes on her, and had not moved. The Senior, who had the ward supper to serve and beds to brush out and backs to rub, not to mention having to make up the emergency bed and clear away the dressings — the Senior tried diplomacy and offered him an orange from her own corner of the medicine closet. He shook his head.

"I guess he wants to know whether that girl from the Avenue's going to get well," said Irish Delia. "He seems to know her."

There was a titter through the ward at this. Old Maggie's gossiping tongue had been busy during the hour. From pity the ward had veered to contempt.

"Humph!" said the Senior, and put the orange back. "Why, yes; I guess she'll get well. But how in Heaven's name am I to let him know?"

She was a resourceful person, however, and by pointing to the Avenue Girl and then nodding reassuringly she got her message of cheer over the gulf of his understanding. In return the Dummy told her by gestures how he knew the girl and how she had bound up the leg of the superintendent's dog. The Senior was a literal person and not occult; and she was very busy. When the Dummy stooped to indicate the dog, a foot or so from the ground, she seized that as the key of the situation.

"He's trying to let me know that he knew her when she was a baby," she observed generally. "All right, if that's the case. Come in and see her when you want to. And now get out, for goodness' sake!"

The Dummy, with his patient shamble, made his way out of the ward and stored his polishes for the night in the corner of a scrub-closet. Then, ignoring supper, he went down the stairs, flight after flight, to the chapel. The late autumn sun had set behind the buildings across the courtyard and the lower part of the silent room was in shadow; but the afterglow came palely through the stained-glass window, with the young John and tall stalks of white lilies, and "To the Memory of My Daughter Elizabeth" beneath.

It was only a coincidence — and not even that to the Dummy — but Elizabeth had been the Avenue Girl's name not so long ago.

The Dummy sat down near the door very humbly and gazed at the memorial window.

<h1 style="text-align:center">II</h1>

Time may be measured in different ways—by joys; by throbs of pain; by instants; by centuries. In a hospital it is marked by night nurses and day nurses; by rounds of the Staff; by visiting days; by medicines and temperatures and milk diets and fever baths; by the distant singing in the chapel on Sundays; by the shift of the morning sun on the east beds to the evening sun on the beds along the west windows.

The Avenue Girl lay alone most of the time. The friendly offices of the ward were not for her. Private curiosity and possible kindliness were over-shadowed by a general arrogance of goodness. The ward flung its virtue at her like a weapon and she raised no defence. In the first days things were not so bad. She lay in shock for a time, and there were not wanting hands during the bad hours to lift a cup of water to her lips; but after that came the tedious time when death no longer hovered overhead and life was there for the asking.

The curious thing was that the Avenue Girl did not ask. She lay for hours without moving, with eyes that seemed tired with looking into the dregs of life. The Probationer was in despair.

"She could get better if she would," she said to the interne one day. The Senior was off duty and they had done the dressing together. "She just won't try."

"Perhaps she thinks it isn't worth while," replied the interne, who was drying his hands carefully while the Probationer waited for the towel.

She was a very pretty Probationer.

"She hasn't much to look forward to, you know."

The Probationer was not accustomed to discussing certain things with young men, but she had the Avenue Girl on her mind.

"She has a home—she admits it." She coloured bravely. "Why—why cannot she go back to it, even now?"

The interne poured a little rosewater and glycerine into the palm of one hand and gave the Probationer the bottle. If his fingers touched hers, she never knew it.

"Perhaps they'd not want her after—well, they'd never feel the same, likely. They'd probably prefer to think of her as dead and let it go at that. There—there doesn't seem to be any way back, you know."

He was exceedingly self-conscious.

"Then life is very cruel," said the Probationer with rather shaky lips.

And going back to the Avenue Girl's bed she filled her cup with ice and straightened her pillows. It was her only way of showing defiance to a world that mutilated its children and turned them out to die. The interne watched her as she worked. It rather galled him to see her touching this patient. He had no particular sympathy for the Avenue Girl. He was a man, and ruthless, as men are apt to be in such things.

The Avenue Girl had no visitors. She had had one or two at first—pretty girls with tired eyes and apologetic glances; a negress who got by the hall porter with a box of cigarettes, which the Senior promptly confiscated; and—the Dummy. Morning and evening came the Dummy and stood by her bed and worshipped. Morning and evening he brought tribute—a flower from the masses that came in daily; an orange, got by no one knows what trickery from the kitchen; a leadpencil; a box of cheap candies. At first the girl had been embarrassed by his visits. Later, as the unfriendliness of the ward grew more pronounced, she greeted him with a faint smile. The first time she smiled he grew quite pale and shuffled out. Late that night they found him sitting in the chapel looking at the window, which was only a blur.

For certain small services in the ward the Senior depended on the convalescents—filling drinking cups; passing milk at eleven and three; keeping the white bedspreads in geometrical order. But the Avenue Girl was taboo. The boycott had been instituted by Old Maggie. The rampant respectability of the ward even went so far as to refuse to wash her in those early morning hours when the night nurse, flying about with her cap on one ear, was carrying tin basins about like a blue-and-white cyclone. The Dummy knew nothing of the washing; the early morning was the time when he polished the brass doorplate which said: Hospital and Free Dispensary. But he knew about the drinking cup and after a time that became his self-appointed task.

On Sundays he put on his one white shirt and a frayed collar two sizes too large and went to chapel. At those times he sat with his prayer book upside down and watched the Probationer who cared for his lady and who had no cap to hide her shining hair, and the interne, who was glad there was no cap because of the hair. God's fool he was, indeed, for he liked to look in the interne'seyes, and did not know an interne cannot marry for years and years, and that a probationer must not upset discipline by being engaged. God's fool, indeed, who could see into the hearts of men, but not into their thoughts or their lives; and who, seeing only thus, on two dimensions of life and not the third, found the Avenue Girl holy and worthy of all worship!

The Probationer worried a great deal.

"It must hurt her so!" she said to the Senior. "Did you see them call that baby away on visiting day for fear she would touch it?"

"None are so good as the untempted," explained the Senior, who had been beautiful and was now placid and full of good works. "You cannot remake the world, child. Bodies are our business here—not souls." But the next moment she called Old Maggie to her.

"I've been pretty patient, Maggie," she said. "You know what I mean. You're the ringleader. Now things are going to change, or—you'll go back on codliver oil to-night."

"Yes'm," said Old Maggie meekly, with hate in her heart. She loathed the codliver oil.

"Go back and straighten her bed!" commanded the Senior sternly.

"Now?"

"Now!"

"It hurts my back to stoop over," whined Old Maggie, with the ward watching. "The doctor said that I— —"

The Senior made a move for the medicine closet and the bottles labelled C.

"I'm going," whimpered Old Maggie. "Can't you give a body time?"

And she went down to defeat, with the laughter of the ward in her ears— down to defeat, for the Avenue Girl would have none of her.

"You get out of here!" she said fiercely as Old Maggie set to work at the draw sheet. "Get out quick—or I'll throw this cup in your face!"

The Senior was watching. Old Maggie put on an air of benevolence and called the Avenue Girl an unlovely name under her breath while she smoothed her pillow. She did not get the cup, but the water out of it, in her hard old face, and matters were as they had been.

The Girl did not improve as she should. The interne did the dressing day after day, while the Probationer helped him—the Senior disliked burned cases—and talked of skin grafting if a new powder he had discovered did no good. Internes are always trying out new things, looking for the great discovery.

The powder did no good. The day came when, the dressing over and the white coverings drawn up smoothly again over her slender body, the Avenue Girl voiced the question that her eyes had asked each time.

"Am I going to lie in this hole all my life?" she demanded.

The interne considered.

"It isn't healing—not very fast anyhow," he said. "If we could get a little skin to graft on you'd be all right in a jiffy. Can't you get some friends to come in? It isn't painful and it's over in a minute."

"Friends? Where would I get friends of that sort?"

"Well, relatives then—some of your own people?"

The Avenue Girl shut her eyes as she did when the dressing hurt her.

"None that I'd care to see," she said. And the Probationer knew she lied. The interne shrugged his shoulders.

"If you think of any let me know. We'll get them here," he said briskly, and turned to see the Probationer rolling up her sleeve.

"Please!" she said, and held out a bare white arm. The interne stared at it stupefied. It was very lovely.

"I am not at all afraid," urged the Probationer, "and my blood is good. It would grow—I know it would."

The interne had hard work not to stoop and kiss the blue veins that rose to the surface in the inner curve of her elbow. The dressing screens were up and the three were quite alone. To keep his voice steady he became stern.

"Put your sleeve down and don't be a foolish girl!" he, commanded. "Put your sleeve down!" His eyes said: "You wonder! You beauty! You brave little girl!"

Because the Probationer seemed to take her responsibilities rather to heart, however, and because, when he should have been thinking of other things, such as calling up the staff and making reports, he kept seeing that white arm and the resolute face above it, the interne worked out a plan.

"I've fixed it, I think," he said, meeting her in a hallway where he had no business to be, and trying to look as if he had not known she was coming. "Father Feeny was in this morning and I tackled him. He's got a lot of students—fellows studying for the priesthood—and he says any daughter of the church shall have skin if he has to flay 'em alive."

"But—is she a daughter of the church?" asked the Probationer. "And even if she were, under the circumstances——"

"What circumstances?" demanded the interne. "Here's a poor girl burned and suffering. The father is not going to ask whether she's of the anointed."

The Probationer was not sure. She liked doing things in the open and with nothing to happen later to make one uncomfortable; but she spoke to the Senior and the Senior was willing. Her chief trouble, after all, was with the Avenue Girl herself.

"I don't want to get well," she said wearily when the thing was put up to her. "What's the use? I'd just go back to the same old thing; and when it got too strong for me I'd end up here again or in the morgue."

"Tell me where your people live, then, and let me send for them."

"Why? To have them read in my face what I've been, and go back home to die of shame?"

The Probationer looked at the Avenue Girl's face.

"There—there is nothing in your face to hurt them," she said, flushing—because there were some things the Probationer had never discussed, even with herself. "You—look sad. Honestly, that's all."

The Avenue Girl held up her thin right hand. The forefinger was still yellow from cigarettes.

"What about that?" she sneered.

"If I bleach it will you let me send for your people?"

"I'll—perhaps," was the most the Probationer could get.

Many people would have been discouraged. Even the Senior was a bit cynical. It took a Probationer still heartsick for home to read in the Avenue Girl's eyes the terrible longing for the things she had given up—for home and home folks; for a clean slate again. The Probationer bleached and scrubbed the finger, and gradually a little of her hopeful spirit touched the other girl.

"What day is it?" the Avenue Girl asked once.

"Friday."

"That's baking day at home. We bake in an out-oven. Did you ever smell bread as it comes from an out-oven?" Or: "That's a pretty shade of blue you nurses wear. It would be nice for working in the dairy, wouldn't it?"

"Fine!" said the Probationer, and scrubbed away to hide the triumph in her eyes.

III

That was the day the Dummy stole the parrot. The parrot belonged to the Girl; but how did he know it? So many things he should have known the Dummy never learned; so many things he knew that he seemed never to have learned! He did not know, for instance, of Father Feeny and the Holy Name students; but he knew of the Avenue Girl's loneliness and heartache, and of the cabal against her. It is one of the black marks on record against him that he refused to polish the plate on Old Maggie's bed, and that he shook his fist at her more than once when the Senior was out of the ward.

And he knew of the parrot. That day, then, a short, stout woman with a hard face appeared in the superintendent's office and demanded a parrot.

"Parrot?" said the superintendent blandly.

"Parrot! That crazy man you keep here walked into my house to-day and stole a parrot—and I want it."

"The Dummy! But what on earth——"

"It was my parrot," said the woman. "It belonged to one of my boarders. She's a burned case up in one of the wards—and she owed me money. I took it for a debt. You call that man and let him look me in the eye while I say parrot to him."

"He cannot speak or hear."

"You call him. He'll understand me!"

They found the Dummy coming stealthily down from the top of the stable and haled him into the office. He was very calm—quite impassive. Apparently he had never seen the woman before; as she raged he smiled cheerfully and shook his head.

"As a matter of fact," said the superintendent, "I don't believe he ever saw the bird; but if he has it we shall find it out and you'll get it again."

They let him go then; and he went to the chapel and looked at a dove above the young John's head. Then he went up to the kitchen and filled his pockets with lettuce leaves. He knew nothing at all of parrots or how to care for them.

Things, you see, were moving right for the Avenue Girl. The stain was coming off—she had been fond of the parrot and now it was close at hand; and Father Feeny's lusty crowd stood ready to come into a hospital ward and shed skin that they generally sacrificed on the football field. But the Avenue Girl had two years to account for—and there was the matter of an alibi.

"I might tell the folks at home anything and they'd believe it because they'd want to believe it," said the Avenue Girl. "But there's the neighbours. I was pretty wild at home. And—there's a fellow who wanted to marry me—he knew how sick I was of the old place and how I wanted my fling. His name was Jerry. We'd have to show Jerry."

The Probationer worried a great deal about this matter of the alibi. It had to be a clean slate for the folks back home, and especially for Jerry. She took her anxieties out walking several times on her off-duty, but nothing seemed to come of it. She walked on the Avenue mostly, because it was near and she could throw a long coat over her blue dress. And so she happened to think of the woman the girl had lived with.

"She got her into all this," thought the Probationer. "She's just got to see her out."

It took three days' off-duty to get her courage up to ringing the doorbell of the house with the bowed shutters, and after she had rung it she wanted very much to run and hide; but she thought of the girl and everything going for nothing for the want of an alibi, and she stuck. The negress opened the door and stared at her.

"She's dead, is she?" she asked.

"No. May I come in? I want to see your mistress."

The negress did not admit her, however. She let her stand in the vestibule and went back to the foot of a staircase.

"One of these heah nurses from the hospital!" she said. "She wants to come in and speak to you."

"Let her in, you fool!" replied a voice from above stairs.

The rest was rather confused. Afterward the Probationer remembered putting the case to the stout woman who had claimed the parrot and finding it difficult to make her understand.

"Don't you see?" she finished desperately. "I want her to go home — to her own folks. She wants it too. But what are we going to say about these last two years?"

The stout woman sat turning over her rings. She was most uncomfortable. After all, what had she done? Had she not warned them again and again about having lighted cigarettes lying round.

"She's in bad shape, is she?"

"She may recover, but she'll be badly scarred — not her face, but her chest and shoulders."

That was another way of looking at it. If the girl was scarred — —

"Just what do you want me to do?" she asked. Now that it was down to brass tacks and no talk about home and mother, she was more comfortable.

"If you could just come over to the hospital while her people are there and — and say she'd lived with you all the time — —"

"That's the truth all right!"

"And—that she worked for you, sewing—she sews very well, she says. And—oh, you'll know what to say; that she's been—all right, you know; anything to make them comfortable and happy."

Now the stout woman was softening—not that she was really hard, but she had developed a sort of artificial veneer of hardness, and good impulses had a hard time crawling through.

"I guess I could do that much," she conceded. "She nursed me when I was down and out with the grippe and that worthless nigger was drunk in the kitchen. But you folks over there have got a parrot that belongs to me. What about that?"

The Probationer knew about the parrot. The Dummy had slipped it into the ward more than once and its profanity had delighted the patients. The Avenue Girl had been glad to see it too; and as it sat on the bedside table and shrieked defiance and oaths the Dummy had smiled benignly. John and the dove—the girl and the parrot!

"I am sorry about the parrot. I—perhaps I could buy him from you."

She got out her shabby little purse, in which she carried her munificent monthly allowance of eight dollars and a little money she had brought from home.

"Twenty dollars takes him. That's what she owed me."

The Probationer had seventeen dollars and eleven cents. She spread it out in her lap and counted it twice.

"I'm afraid that's all," she said. She had hoped the second count would show up better. "I could bring the rest next month."

The Probationer folded the money together and held it out. The stout woman took it eagerly.

"He's yours," she said largely. "Don't bother about the balance. When do you want me?"

"I'll send you word," said the Probationer, and got up. She was almost dizzy with excitement and the feeling of having no money at all in the world and a parrot she did not want. She got out into the air somehow and back to the hospital. She took a bath immediately and put on everything fresh, and felt much better—but very poor. Before she went on duty she said a little prayer about thermometers—that she should not break hers until she had money for a new one.

Father Feeny came and lined up six budding priests outside the door of the ward. He was a fine specimen of manhood and he had asked no questions at all. The Senior thought she had better tell him something, but he put up a white hand.

"What does it matter, sister?" he said cheerfully. "Yesterday is gone and to-day is a new day. Also there is to-morrow"—his Irish eyes twinkled—"and a fine day it will be by the sunset."

Then he turned to his small army.

"Boys," he said, "it's a poor leader who is afraid to take chances with his men. I'm going first"—he said fir-rst. "It's a small thing, as I've told you—a bit of skin and it's over. Go in smiling and come out smiling! Are you ready, sir?" This to the interne.

That was a great day in the ward. The inmates watched Father Feeny and the interne go behind the screens, both smiling, and they watched the father come out very soon after, still smiling but a little bleached. And they watched the line patiently waiting outside the door, shortening one by one. After a time the smiles were rather forced, as if waiting was telling on them; but there was no deserter—only one six-foot youth, walking with a swagger to contribute his little half inch or so of cuticle, added a sensation to the general excitement by fainting halfway up the ward; and he remained in blissful unconsciousness until it was all over.

Though the interne had said there was no way back, the first step had really been taken; and he was greatly pleased with himself and with everybody because it had been his idea. The Probationer tried to find a chance to thank him; and, failing that, she sent a grateful little note to his room:

Is Mimi the Austrian to have a baked apple?

[Signed]   WARD A.

P.S.—It went through wonderfully! She is so cheerful since it is over. How can I ever thank you?

The reply came back very quickly:

Baked apple, without milk, for Mimi. WARD A.

[Signed]   D. L. S.

P.S.—Can you come up on the roof for a little air?

She hesitated over that for some time. A really honest-to-goodness nurse may break a rule now and then and nothing happen; but a probationer is only on trial and has to be exceedingly careful—though any one might go to the roof and watch the sunset. She decided not to go. Then she pulled her soft hair down over her forehead, where it was most becoming, and fastened it with tiny hairpins, and went up after all—not because she intended to, but because as she came out of her room the elevator was going up—not down. She was on the roof almost before she knew it.

The interne was there in fresh white ducks, smoking. At first they talked of skin grafting and the powder that had not done what was expected of it. After a time, when the autumn twilight had fallen on them like a benediction, she took her courage in her hands and told of her visit to the house on the Avenue, and about the parrot and the plot.

The interne stood very still. He was young and intolerant. Some day he would mellow and accept life as it is—not as he would have it. When she had finished he seemed to have drawn himself into a shell, turtle fashion, and huddled himself together. The shell was pride and old prejudice and the intolerance of youth. "She had to have an alibi!" said the Probationer.

"Oh, of course," very stiffly.

"I cannot see why you disapprove. Something had to be done."

"I cannot see that you had to do it; but it's your own affair, of course. Only——"

"Please go on."

"Well, one cannot touch dirt without being soiled."

"I think you will be sorry you said that," said the Probationer stiffly. And she went down the staircase, leaving him alone. He was sorry, of course; but he would not say so even to himself. He thought of the Probationer, with her eager eyes and shining hair and her warm little heart, ringing the bell of the Avenue house and making her plea—and his blood ran hot in him. It was just then that the parrot spoke on the other side of the chimney.

"Gimme a bottle of beer!" it said. "Nice cold beer! Cold beer!"

The interne walked furiously toward the sound. Must this girl of the streets and her wretched associates follow him everywhere? She had ruined his life already. He felt that it was ruined. Probably the Probationer would never speak to him again.

The Dummy was sitting on a bench, with the parrot on his knee looking rather queer from being smuggled about under a coat and fed the curious things that the Dummy thought a bird should eat. It had a piece of apple pie in its claw now.

"Cold beer!" said the parrot, and eyed the interne crookedly.

The Dummy had not heard him, of course. He sat looking over the parapet toward the river, with one knotted hand smoothing the bird's ruffled plumage and such a look of wretchedness in his eyes that it hurt to see it. God's fools, who cannot reason, can feel. Some instinct of despair had seized him for its own—some conception, perhaps, of what life would never mean to him. Before it, the interne's wrath gave way to impotency.

"Cold beer!" said the parrot wickedly.

<h1 style="text-align:center">IV</h1>

The Avenue Girl improved slowly. Morning and evening came the Dummy and smiled down at her, with reverence in his eyes. She could smile back now and sometimes she spoke to him. There was a change in the Avenue Girl. She was less sullen. In the back of her eyes each morning found a glow of hope — that died, it is true, by noontime; but it came again with the new day.

"How's Polly this morning, Montmorency?" she would say, and give him a bit of toast from her breakfast for the bird. Or: "I wish you could talk, Reginald. I'd like to hear what Rose said when you took the parrot. It must have been a scream!"

He brought her the first chrysanthemums of the fall and laid them on her pillow. It was after he had gone, while the Probationer was combing out the soft short curls of her hair, that she mentioned the Dummy. She strove to make her voice steady, but there were tears in her eyes.

"The old goat's been pretty good to me, hasn't he?" she said.

"I believe it is very unusual. I wonder" — the Probationer poised the comb — "perhaps you remind him of some one he used to know."

They knew nothing, of course, of the boy John and the window.

"He's about the first decent man I ever knew," said the Avenue Girl — "and he's a fool!"

"Either a fool or very, very wise," replied the Probationer.

The interne and the Probationer were good friends again, but they had never quite got back to the place they had lost on the roof. Over the Avenue Girl's dressing their eyes met sometimes, and there was an appeal in the man's and tenderness; but there was pride too. He would not say he had not meant it. Any man will tell you that he was entirely right, and that she had been most unwise and needed a good scolding — only, of course, it is never the wise people who make life worth the living.

And an important thing had happened — the Probationer had been accepted and had got her cap. She looked very stately in it, though it generally had a dent somewhere from her forgetting she had it on and putting her hat on over it. The first day she wore it she knelt at prayers with the others, and said a little Thank You! for getting through when she was so unworthy. She asked to be made clean and pure, and delivered from vanity, and of some use in the world. And, trying to think of the things she had been remiss in, she went out that night in a rain and bought some seed and things for the parrot.

Prodigal as had been Father Feeny and his battalion, there was more grafting needed before the Avenue Girl could take her scarred body and soul out into the world again. The Probationer offered, but was refused politely.

"You are a part of the institution now," said the interne, with his eyes on her cap. He was rather afraid of the cap. "I cannot cripple the institution."

It was the Dummy who solved that question. No one knew how he knew the necessity or why he had not come forward sooner; but come he did and would not be denied. The interne went to a member of the staff about it.

"The fellow works round the house," he explained; "but he's taken a great fancy to the girl and I hardly know what to do."

"My dear boy," said the staff, "one of the greatest joys in the world is to suffer for a woman. Let him go to it."

So the Dummy bared his old-young arm — not once, but many times. Always as the sharp razor nicked up its bit of skin he looked at the girl and smiled. In the early evening he perched the parrot on his bandaged arm and sat on the roof or by the fountain in the courtyard. When the breeze blew strong enough the water flung over the rim and made little puddles in the hollows of the cement pavement. Here belated sparrows drank or splashed their dusty feathers, and the parrot watched them crookedly.

The Avenue Girl grew better with each day, but remained wistful-eyed. The ward no longer avoided her, though she was never one of them. One day the Probationer found a new baby in the children's ward; and, with the passion of maternity that is the real reason for every good woman's being, she cuddled the mite in her arms. She visited the nurses in the different wards.

"Just look!" she would say, opening her arms. "If I could only steal it!"

The Senior, who had once been beautiful and was now calm and placid, smiled at her. Old Maggie must peer and cry out over the child. Irish Delia must call down a blessing on it. And so up the ward to the Avenue Girl; the Probationer laid the baby in her arms.

"Just a minute," she explained. "I'm idling and I have no business to. Hold it until I give the three o'clocks." Which means the three-o'clock medicines.

When she came back the Avenue Girl had a new look in her eyes; and that day the little gleam of hope, that usually died, lasted and grew.

At last came the day when the alibi was to be brought forward. The girl had written home and the home folks were coming. In his strange way the Dummy knew that a change was near. The kaleidoscope would shift again and the Avenue Girl would join the changing and disappearing figures that fringed the inner circle of his heart.

One night he did not go to bed in the ward bed that was his only home, beside the little stand that held his only possessions. The watchman missed him and found him asleep in the chapel in one of the seats, with the parrot drowsing on the altar.

Rose—who was the stout woman—came early. She wore a purple dress, with a hat to match, and purple gloves. The ward eyed her with scorn and a certain deference. She greeted the Avenue Girl effusively behind the screens that surrounded the bed.

"Well, you do look pinched!" she said. "Ain't it a mercy it didn't get to your face! Pretty well chewed up, aren't you?"

"Do you want to see it?"

"Good land! No! Now look here, you've got to put me wise or I'll blow the whole thing. What's my little stunt? The purple's all right for it, isn't it?"

"All you need to do," said the Avenue Girl wearily, "is to say that I've been sewing for you since I came to the city. And—if you can say anything good——"

"I'll do that all right," Rose affirmed. She put a heavy silver bag on the bedside table and lowered herself into a chair. "You leave it to me, dearie. There ain't anything I won't say."

The ward was watching with intense interest. Old Maggie, working the creaking bandage machine, was palpitating with excitement. From her chair by the door she could see the elevator and it was she who announced the coming of destiny.

"Here comes the father," she confided to the end of the ward. "Guess the mother couldn't come."

It was not the father though. It was a young man who hesitated in the doorway, hat in hand—a tall young man, with a strong and not unhandsome face. The Probationer, rather twitchy from excitement and anxiety, felt her heart stop and race on again. Jerry, without a doubt!

The meeting was rather constrained. The girl went whiter than her pillows and half closed her eyes; but Rose, who would have been terrified at the sight of an elderly farmer, was buoyantly relieved and at her ease.

"I'm sorry," said Jerry. "I—we didn't realise it had been so bad. The folks are well; but—I thought I'd better come. They're expecting you back home."

"It was nice of you to come," said the girl, avoiding his eyes. "I—I'm getting along fine."

"I guess introductions ain't necessary," put in Rose briskly. "I'm Mrs. Sweeney. She's been living with me—working for me, sewing. She's sure a fine sewer! She made this suit I'm wearing."

Poor Rose, with "custom made" on every seam of the purple! But Jerry was hardly listening. His eyes were on the girl among the pillows.

"I see," said Jerry slowly. "You haven't said yet, Elizabeth. Are you going home?"

"If—they want me."

"Of course they want you!" Again Rose: "Why shouldn't they? You've been a good girl and a credit to any family. If they say anything mean to you you let me know."

"They'll not be mean to her. I'm sure they'll want to write and thank you. If you'll just give me your address, Mrs. Sweeney——"

He had a pencil poised over a notebook. Rose hesitated. Then she gave her address on the Avenue, with something of bravado in her voice. After all, what could this country-store clerk know of the Avenue? Jerry wrote it down carefully.

"Sweeney—with an e?" he asked politely.

"With three e's," corrected Rose, and got up with dignity.

"Well, good-bye, dearie," she said. "You've got your friends now and you don't need me. I guess you've had your lesson about going to sleep with a cig—about being careless with fire. Drop me a postal when you get the time."

She shook hands with Jerry and rustled and jingled down the ward, her chin well up. At the door she encountered Old Maggie, her arms full of bandages.

"How's the Avenue?" asked Old Maggie.

Rose, however, like all good actresses, was still in the part as she made her exit. She passed Old Maggie unheeding, severe respectability in every line of her figure, every nod of her purple plumes. She was still in the part when she encountered the Probationer.

"It's going like a house afire!" she said. "He swallowed it all—hook and bait! And—oh, yes, I've got something for you." She went down into her silver bag and pulled out a roll of bills. "I've felt meaner'n a dog every time I've thought of you buying that parrot. I've got a different view of life— maybe—from yours; but I'm not taking candy from a baby."

When the Probationer could speak Rose was taking herself and the purple into the elevator and waving her a farewell.

"Good-bye!" she said. "If ever you get stuck again just call on me."

With Rose's departure silence fell behind the screen. The girl broke it first.

"They're all well, are they?"

"All well. Your mother's been kind of poorly. She thought you'd write to her." The girl clenched her hands under the bedclothing. She could not speak just then. "There's nothing much happened. The post office burned down last summer. They're building a new one. And—I've been building. I tore down the old place."

"Are you going to be married, Jerry?"

"Some day, I suppose. I'm not worrying about it. It was something to do; it kept me from—thinking."

The girl looked at him and something gripped her throat. He knew! Rose might have gone down with her father, but Jerry knew! Nothing was any use. She knew his rigid morality, his country-bred horror of the thing she was. She would have to go back—to Rose and the others. He would never take her home.

Down at the medicine closet the Probationer was carbolising thermometers and humming a little song. Everything was well. The Avenue Girl was with her people and at seven o'clock the Probationer was going to the roof—to meet some one who was sincerely repentant and very meek.

In the convalescent ward next door they were singing softly—one of those spontaneous outbursts that have their origin in the hearts of people and a melody all their own:

'Way down upon de S'wanee Ribber,

   Far, far away,

Dere's wha my heart is turnin' ebber—

   Dere's wha de old folks stay.

It penetrated back of the screen, where the girl lay in white wretchedness—and where Jerry, with death in his eyes, sat rigid in his chair.

"Jerry?"

"Yes."

"I—I guess I've been pretty far away."

"Don't tell me about it!" A cry, this.

"You used to care for me, Jerry. I'm not expecting that now; but if you'd only believe me when I say I'm sorry——"

"I believe you, Elizabeth."

"One of the nurses here says——Jerry, won't you look at me?" With some difficulty he met her eyes. "She says that because one starts wrong one needn't go wrong always. I was ashamed to write. She made me do it."

She held out an appealing hand, but he did not take it. All his life he had built up a house of morality. Now his house was crumbling and he stood terrified in the wreck. "It isn't only because I've been hurt that I—am sorry," she went on. "I loathed it! I'd have finished it all long ago, only—I was afraid."

"I would rather have found you dead!"

There is a sort of anesthesia of misery. After a certain amount of suffering the brain ceases to feel. Jerry watched the white curtain of the screen swaying in the wind, settled his collar, glanced at his watch. He was quite white. The girl's hand still lay on the coverlet. Somewhere back in the numbed brain that would think only little thoughts he knew that if he touched that small, appealing hand the last wall of his house would fall.

It was the Dummy, after all, who settled that for him. He came with his afternoon offering of cracked ice just then and stood inside the screen, staring. Perhaps he had known all along how it would end, that this, his saint, would go—and not alone—to join the vanishing circle that had ringed the inner circle of his heart. Just at the time it rather got him. He swayed a little and clutched at the screen; but the next moment he had placed the bowl on the stand and stood smiling down at the girl.

"The only person in the world who believes in me!" said the girl bitterly. "And he's a fool!"

The Dummy smiled into her eyes. In his faded, childish eyes there was the eternal sadness of his kind, eternal tenderness, and the blur of one who has looked much into a far distance. Suddenly he bent over and placed the man's hand over the girl's.

The last wall was down! Jerry buried his face in the white coverlet.

The interne was pacing the roof anxiously. Golden sunset had faded to lavender — to dark purple — to night.

The Probationer came up at last — not a probationer now, of course; but she had left off her cap and was much less stately.

"I'm sorry," she explained; "but I've been terribly busy. It went off so well!"

"Of course — if you handled it."

"You know — don't you? — it was the lover who came. He looks so strong and good — oh, she is safe now!"

"That's fine!" said the interne absently. They were sitting on the parapet now and by sliding his hand along he found her fingers. "Isn't it a glorious evening?" He had the fingers pretty close by that time; and suddenly gathering them up he lifted the hand to his lips.

"Such a kind little hand!" he said over it. "Such a dear, tender little hand! My hand!" he said, rather huskily.

Down in the courtyard the Dummy sat with the parrot on his knee. At his feet the superintendent's dog lay on his side and dreamed of battle. The Dummy's eyes lingered on the scar the Avenue Girl had bandaged — how long ago!

His eyes wandered to the window with the young John among the lilies. In the stable were still the ambulance horses that talked to him without words. And he had the parrot. If he thought at all it was that his Father was good and that, after all, he was not alone. The parrot edged along his knee and eyed him with saturnine affection.

www.ingramcontent.com/pod-product-compliance
Lightning Source LLC
Chambersburg PA
CBHW080908190726
48294CB00008B/2013